DECODE

DECLAN REEDE: THE UNTOLD STORY (EXTRA NOVELLA)

MICHELLE IRWIN

Michelle
xxx.

COPYRIGHT

DEDICATION:

Because too much Declan is never enough, and we all want to know how far he's come.

For you, Declan, and your family.

DECLAN REEDE: THE UNTOLD STORY

CONTENTS:

GLOSSARY:

Note: This book is set in Australia, as such it uses Australian/UK spelling and some Australian slang. Although you should be able to understand the novel without a glossary, there is always fun to be had in learning new words. Temperatures are in Celsius, weight is in kilograms, and distance is (generally) in kilometres (although we still have some slang which uses miles).

Arse: Ass.

AVO: Apprehended Violence Order.

Bedhead: Headboard.

Bench: Counter.

Bitumen: Asphalt.

Bonnet: Hood.

Boot: Trunk.

Bottle-o: Bottle shop/liquor store.

Buggery: Multiple meanings. Technically bugger/buggery is sodomy/anal sex, but in Australia, the use is more varied. Bugger is a common expression of disbelief/disapproval.

Came down in the last shower (Do you think I): Born yesterday

CAMS: Confederation of Australian Motor Sport.

Cherry (Drag racing): Red light indicating that you "red-lighted"/jumped the start.

Cock-ups: Fuck-ups/mistakes.

Dagwood Dogs: Corndogs

Diamante: Rhinestone.

Dipper: See S Bends below.

Do (Charity Do): Function/event.

Dob: Tell on.

Doona: Blanket/comforter.

Fairy-Floss: Cotton candy.

Fillies: Girls.

Footpath: Sidewalk.

Formal: Prom.

Fours: Cars with a four-cylinder engine.

HANS: Head And Neck Support.
Loo: Toilet.
Message bank: Voicemail.
Mirena: An IUD that contains and releases a small amount of a progesterone hormone directly into the uterus.
Mozzies: Mosquitoes.
Necked: Drank from.
Newsagency: A shop which sells newspapers/magazines/lotto tickets. Similar to a convenience store, but without the food.
Off my face: Drunk/under the influence (including of drugs).
Pap: Paparazzi.
Panadol/Paracetamol: Active ingredient in pain-relievers like Tylenol and Panadol.
Pavlova: Meringue-based desert, usually served covered with fresh cream and seasonal fruits (aka: sugar heaven).
Phone/Mobile Phone/Mobile Number: Cell/cell phone/cell number.
Prep (school): Preparation year.
Privateer: Someone who finances their own races.
Real Estate: All-inclusive term meaning real estate agency/property management firm.
Rego: Registration (general); cost of vehicle licence.
Ricer: Someone who drives a hotted up four-cylinder (usually imported) car, and makes modifications to make it (and make it look) faster.
Rugby League: One of the codes of football played in Australia.
S bends (and into the Dipper): Part of the racetrack shaped into an S shape. On Bathurst track, the Dipper is the biggest of the S bends, so called because there used to be a dip in the road there before track resurfacing made it safer.
Sandwich with the lot: Sandwich with the works.
Schoolies: Week-long (or more) celebration for year twelves graduating school. Similar to spring break. The Gold Coast is a popular destination for school leavers from all around the country, and they usually have a number of organised events, including alcohol-free events as a percentage of school leavers are usually

under eighteen (the legal drinking age in Australia).

Scrag: Whore/slut.

Scrutineering: Process of going over the car and rules to ensure there is no corruption or mistakes.

Shout (referring to drinks or food): Buy for someone. "Get the tab."

Silly Season: Off season in sports. Primarily where most of the trades happen (e.g. driver's moving teams, sponsorship changes etc).

Skerrick: Scrap.

Slicks: A special type of racing tyre with no tread. They're designed to get the maximum amount of surface on the road at all times. Wet weather tyres have chunky tread to displace the water from the track.

Skulled: (can also be spelled sculled and skolled) Chugged/Drank everything in the bottle/glass.

Soft Drinks: Soda/pop.

Stiff Shit: Tough shit/too bad.

Sunnies: Sunglasses.

TAFE: (Technical And Further Education) Trade school

Tassie: Tasmania (in the same way Aussie = Australia)

Taxi: Cab.

Thrummed: Hummed/vibrated.

Tossers: Pricks/assholes/jerks.

Tyres: Tires.

Year Twelve: Senior.

Wag: Ditch school.

Wank: Masturbate

Wankers: Tossers/Jerk-offs.

Weet-Bix: Breakfast cereal brand.

Whinge: Whine/complain.

Uni: University/college.

CHAPTER ONE

SANTA BABY

THE LEAD-UP TO my second Christmas with my little family was filled with anticipation. So much had changed in the year and a bit we'd been together; some good, some bad, but very little that I would alter if given the opportunity. For Christmas, we were staying put in our house in Sydney, mostly because it was the last we'd have in the space, and Alyssa's family was coming to visit us. Because they weren't arriving until Boxing Day, we were free to spend Christmas Eve and the following morning however we wanted.

With Phoebe already safely tucked up in bed, there was little I had left to do but wait for eleven o'clock because I'd been given explicit instructions not to be in our bedroom until then. Apparently, Alyssa still needed to wrap my present. When I finished doing the Daddy/Santa thing, I checked the time again. I had another fifteen minutes to kill.

I turned off the Christmas tree lights, checked the locks, ate the cookies, and drank the milk left in the fridge for the man in red. At exactly eleven o'clock, I knocked on the bedroom door.

"Can I come in?" I asked quietly.

There was no answer from within so I pushed the door open. The room was darkened except for the slight flicker of candlelight as the quiet notes of a pop song played over the stereo speakers.

"Alyssa?" I called as I took in the scene. The bed was immaculately made with red and white sheets. A pair of red boxer shorts with white fur trim around the waist and legs hung over the foot of the bed, with a Santa hat resting on top of them. As I drew closer, I saw a note that read, *Shower, shave, and put these on*.

As I gathered up the shorts, I tried to work out what song was playing, but it was so low I couldn't really hear it, only the rhythmic baseline.

I tried the door to the en suite, but it was locked. Small sounds—banging and shifting—echoed from within. I could have broken in to the room easily enough if I'd needed to, but Alyssa never locked the door when she showered, so I knew she wanted her privacy for some reason. I left the bedroom and showered in the main bathroom. I wanted to follow the instructions on the note, trusting Alyssa enough to know that if I did as requested, good things were bound to follow.

I dried quickly and then slipped on the boxer shorts. The white fur tickled the sensitive skin of my stomach and upper thighs. There was nothing I could do about the tent forming inside the shorts, but I figured Alyssa wouldn't mind. In fact, I was sure she was counting on it.

Lastly, I slipped the Santa hat over my still damp auburn hair.

I headed back to the bedroom with a lump growing in my throat to match the one in my pants.

What does she have planned?

A new note was on the end of the bed. *Lie down.*

I did as she requested, moving onto the middle of the bed and resting back on my elbows so that I had a better view of the en suite door. The music had changed, but it was still too quiet to work out the song.

Alyssa came out of the bathroom, dressed in a long bathrobe. I strained to see her in the low light while I waited for my eyes to adjust. She didn't even look over at the bed as she headed to the stereo, but she knew I was there. My breathing was so loud and rough with desire that the neighbours could probably have pinpointed my location in the house.

The music flared and a jazz-style rhythm poured out of the speakers. Alyssa pulled on a Santa hat and dropped her bathrobe. I had no trouble noticing what she'd previously hidden from my view.

She wore a set of panties that matched my boxers, except with the trim only around the waist, not around her legs. Covering her chest and waist was a sheer red baby-doll nightie with matching white trim. Her cleavage blossomed over the top of the closure. A slit down the centre of the garment gave me a peek at the tantalizing skin beneath. Sheer white stockings wrapped her legs and red high heels adorned her feet.

I swallowed loudly as I drank in the sight of her. What had been a tent before quickly morphed into a multi-story apartment building as my cock strained to get closer to her.

"Oh, Santa," she murmured as her eyes roamed hungrily over my body. "I didn't realise you'd be home from your rounds so early." She pouted. "I haven't even finished getting dressed."

In the moment it took me to compose myself enough to speak, I recognised the lyrics to the song playing on the stereo and had to smirk at her choice of "Santa Baby."

I almost chuckled at the thought of being seduced to the accompaniment of a Christmas carol, but the absolutely earnest look on Alyssa's face stopped me.

"I, umm . . . I don't mind," I murmured to her as I stretched one arm out to her in invitation.

"But I've been trying so *hard* to be on the good list." The way she said the word *hard* sent a message straight down to my groin.

"Hmmm, you have been rather *naughty* this year, haven't you?"

She nodded and took one step closer to me. "You wouldn't believe some of the things I've done this year."

"Santa sees everything," I told her, my voice low and needful.

She giggled. "Oh, I hope not. Otherwise he'd be a dirty perve." Her fingers traced the line of the fur edging her breasts.

My fingers twitched with longing to touch them myself.

I quirked my eyebrow at her and patted my lap. "Well, just for the sake of not ruining Santa's reputation, why don't you sit in my lap and tell me what you've done that is so naughty?"

She took a step closer. "I've had improper thoughts about someone."

I couldn't stop my grin. "That's not so bad. You can't control your thoughts, only your actions."

She inched closer until her thighs were resting on the bed. "I've touched myself," she whispered. "Down there." Her fingertips trailed along her stomach before brushing against her pussy.

I gulped. She knew precisely what she was doing to me. I was surprised I had the willpower to stay on the bed rather than throwing myself at her and claiming her roughly.

The mattress dipped as she climbed onto the bed, crawling across it until she was straddling my stomach. She put her lips alongside my ear. Her hot breath caressed the side of my face as she whispered, "I've even seduced a married man, and I plan on doing that over and over."

I was beyond words and groaned out something incoherent.

Her nose skimmed along my chin before her lips pressed softly to the column of my throat. Her heat permeated through her panties onto my stomach. I longed for her to sit just a little further south.

She licked and sucked on my throat for another couple of seconds, while my hands reached up under her sheer outfit and ran along the smooth skin of her back. Before long, her mouth was back near my ear. Her voice, soft and breathy, teased me. "I'd do anything to get back on the good list."

Her words radiated through me. "Anything?" I repeated with as much volume as I could muster.

"*Anything*," she declared lustfully.

"Fuck me!" I growled. We might have been apart for four years only to reunite little more than twelve months ago, but she knew exactly what to do to reduce me to a puddle of need and desire.

A mocking grin played on her luscious lips. "Oh, I plan to. Just not *quite* yet."

She planted delicate, nerve-shattering kisses down my chest, sliding her sensuous body along mine until her knees rested near my shins. I watched her the whole way, knowing these would be images I would recall frequently on lonely nights to come. She teased the fur trim around my waist slowly, dipping her fingers underneath and stroking my skin. I threw my head back and collapsed onto the bed.

Her mouth teased and tortured me a few minutes longer before her wanton fingers slid underneath my boxers and dragged them slowly off. The fur trim tickled as it grazed my rock-hard cock. Seconds later, warmth and wetness replaced the soft texture.

I pushed myself up on one elbow and was blessed with the sight of Alyssa's perfect lips wrapped around my dick. A strangled murmur of absolute pleasure escaped me as she sucked my full length into her mouth. I dug my fingers into her silky hair. My strokes matching the rhythm of her mouth as she drew me in deeply. Her tongue caressed my length inside her mouth, swirling across the tip whenever she pulled back.

"Fuck, you're beautiful," I whispered with reverence. I was still amazed that she was mine; wholly and solely mine.

She laughed softly around my length, the vibrations of her throat sending tremors through my body. If she kept up the same pace, I wouldn't last long. I placed a shaky hand on her shoulder and released a series of grunts and groans that were meant to resemble, "Stop, Lys, or I'll come."

I offered her my hand and gently coaxed her back up my body. When she reached my mouth, I flipped her over and began to trace the lines of her body I'd been fantasising about since my first glimpse of her outfit. My tongue trailed along the curve of her breasts, and I rubbed my nose softly against the white fur resting against her collarbone.

As I explored her body, my hips ground into her. The sensation of the soft fur on her panties rubbing against my stomach each time I thrust forward threatened to undo me.

From the sounds she made, I was certain she had no complaints about the feeling either.

After peeling her underwear away, I trailed my fingers across her pussy. My tongue traced along her once before pressing her open with my fingers. When her hips arched, I slid my fingers into her wetness as my tongue brushed across her clit.

Moving upward with my mouth, I kissed a trail up her stomach and onto her breasts, shifting the material out of my way as I went. My dick begged for some attention, so I removed my fingers and climbed up her body.

I longed for her so badly.

Wrapping my fingers in her hair, I kissed her throat and chest as I pushed inside her. With each thrust, moans of ecstasy escaped her lips. I kissed her sweetly, enjoying every second of my time loving her

The nightgown, although sheer, obstructed my view. I unclasped it, revealing her perfect breasts. I kissed my way around her chest, moving steadily and lavishing attention on both nipples equally. She writhed and bucked into me. It was my cue to move a little faster. A little harder. A little deeper. I continued to love her body while rocking into the heaven resting between her legs.

I wasn't going to last much longer, and I didn't want to come so soon, so I flipped us again, granting her control. The sight of her above me, her lips plump and full from our kisses, the swell of her breasts rocking in time to our movements, it all sent me into overdrive and made me change my mind about it being better with her on top.

On top of me or underneath, she was still driving me to oblivion far too fast.

Sitting up, I grabbed her hips to guide her up my body. At first she seemed a little confused, but she went along with my silent directions anyway. I helped her onto her knees before grabbing her arse cheeks with my hands, dipping my head, and sucking on her clit.

"Oh, my fucking God!" she exclaimed as her hands found my hair and pressed my face further into her.

With the angle afforded by the new position, I was able to reach different spots with my tongue. I worshipped her with my mouth until she came apart above me.

Once her elbows buckled and I supported the bulk of her weight, I pushed her down my body a little and slid her over me again. I sat upright and wrapped her body around me, rocking her hips with my hands.

This time when I was close, I had no desire to stop. At least I'd sent Alyssa to heaven before it was over—that was all that mattered. I clutched her arse tightly and bit into her shoulder lightly as I came with a rush.

After my body had stopped pulsating, I collapsed back onto the bed, pulling Alyssa with me. Eventually, my breathing recovered enough to allow me to talk. "I've never had so much fun unwrapping a present before."

She giggled and then whispered, "That wasn't your present."

I pushed her off me a little to inspect her expression. "What?"

"You don't get your present until Christmas."

I pouted, but then I looked over at the clock. "It's past midnight."

She grinned and sat upright. "You're right. Thank goodness for that, 'cause keeping this secret is killing me."

I furrowed my brow in confusion. She climbed off the bed, refastening the sheer red number as she went. She disappeared into the bathroom. When she returned, she had a small, long box in her hand, about the right size for a watch. It was wrapped in gold paper and had a big purple bow on it.

I unwrapped it carefully, watching her expression as I did. It showed her excitement, but there was also a trace of apprehension around the corners of her eyes.

Once I'd made my way down to the box itself, I gently pulled the lid off and then peered inside. It took me a second to understand exactly what I saw nestled amongst the tissue paper.

A tiny stick.

A plastic strip with two pink bars.

Once it had dawned on me, I couldn't stop the smile from

crossing my face.

"Really?" I asked, wondering if her smile at the Christmas party a few days earlier when we'd heard Morgan and Eden were expecting had held a few more secrets than my own.

She nodded.

I glanced down again as if expecting everything to be different when I did. But the gift was there, unchanged. The positive pregnancy test. "We're having another baby?"

"Are you sure it's what you want?" she asked, apprehension clear in her voice.

"Fuck, Lys, I can't think of a time I've ever had a better Christmas present," I said as I pulled her tightly against my chest. "Except maybe last year when you said yes to being my wife."

CHAPTER TWO

PLAYING FAVOURITES

THE SQUEAL ECHOED through the empty house too early in the morning.

I shifted my arm off my face and checked the clock beside the bed.

Fuck, it wasn't even four yet.

After our post-midnight bedtime, it was far too early to be awake. The door to our bedroom swung open seconds after the squeal cut off and then Phoebe was flying through the air onto our bed. When I saw her trajectory—about level with Alyssa's stomach—I shot up from the bed to catch her. The last thing I wanted was for her to accidentally hurt the baby.

It was far too fucking early in the morning for pre-schooler football, and I nearly dislocated my shoulder with my fumbling catch. Better that than letting Phoebe land on Alyssa, though. After wrestling her to the bed, my fingers tickled her squishy little sides until she squealed.

"Hey, princess, why are you in here so early?"

She climbed to her feet and started bouncing on the bed. "Santa came. Santa came."

"Phoebe, don't—" Alyssa's sleepy voice cut off with a moan as she pushed herself up. She clamped her hand over her mouth and gagged before swallowing hard and sucking down a breath. When she took her hand away, she continued, "Don't jump on the bed please, sweetie."

Phoebe bounced once more and then landed hard on her knees, just inches from Alyssa's belly. I gasped when she landed. I uttered a quiet, "Careful."

Worried that she might accidentally hurt the baby if she kept jumping on the bed, I grabbed Phoebe again and helped her onto the floor.

"Mummy isn't feeling too good," I said before offering to take Phoebe to her room so she could show me what Santa brought her for Christmas. When I glanced back at Alyssa, she was trying not to laugh. I'd have to ask her why later.

Phoebe led me into her bedroom and showed me the doll's house and racetrack she'd gotten. Alyssa and I had a bet over which would end up being her favourite toy. Of course, Alyssa didn't know I'd tipped the scales in my favour by calling in reinforcements in the form of miniature versions of the stickers from my Bathurst race to go on the slot cars. Phoebe had loved it when I'd placed third in that race, so it gave me an unfair advantage.

Watching Phoebe show me her dolls and her car that was "just like Daddy's," my memory turned to my podium finish at that race. Because Dane Kent, my co-driver, had slipped into the car my rival, Hunter Blake, had vacated, Sinclair Racing hadn't needed the car back and I'd been able to race once more as a privateer.

The last race of the year, the one at Homebush Stadium near Sydney, was a solo race. It offered me one last chance to stretch my legs before taking over at Wood Racing the following year.

It was during planning for the Homebush that Paige Wood, the owner of Wood Racing, and I had started our negotiations. Although in truth, our first "negotiation" consisted of little more than her snarling at me and hanging up the second I'd spoken.

Apparently, she still wasn't over our run-in on New Year's Eve or the fact that I'd taken a lower paying, less glorified position at Sinclair over the one she'd offered me.

Once Alyssa had taken over negotiations and started talking dollars though, Paige came to the party pretty fucking quickly. Especially after Alyssa detailed a decent settlement and handover period, the sponsorship deals she already had lined up, and offered a profit share lasting until the day Paige handed the reins to us fully.

It might have seemed like we were giving Paige far too much, and we were sure that's why she jumped at the sale, but in reality, it was all to protect our investment. I might've jagged it at Bathurst, but I wasn't nearly fucking ready to run a race team single-handedly—especially not when I still had my apprenticeship to finish and a car to drive.

Despite the hole she'd dug for herself in trying to court me onto her fucking team, Paige wasn't stupid. She'd run a successful team, and had helped her father do it in the years before that. Much as I hated to admit it, there was some shit I could learn from her. By sharing the profits for the first few years, we would keep Paige motivated to earn maximum dollars.

By the time the month-long negotiations ended—after email chains that would rival *War and Peace* for length—everyone was happy; including Danny Sinclair, my former boss and now silent partner.

After all, it'd been my work that had seen Dane Kent back in a Sinclair Racing car and left Danny able to claim a partial stake in Paige's company.

"Daddy, did you see the dolly?" Phoebe said, drawing me back to the present as she handed me one of the dolls from inside the doll's house. "It looks like Mummy."

When I saw the hair and eye colours, it grew clear that Alyssa had some tricks up her sleeve too. "It does. It's pretty just like her."

"She's my favourite dolly." Phoebe hugged her doll to her chest.

"Did Santa bring you that?" Alyssa asked from the doorway,

smiling over the top of her cup of tea.

"Yeah, he did." She dropped the doll and picked up the slot car. "And he gaved me this too!"

Alyssa grabbed the car from her, raising her brow at me when she saw the stickers it was decked out with. I nodded toward the doll with my own cynical glare.

She smirked into her mug, confirming my suspicion that she was playing as dirty as I had when it came to the Christmas game.

Phoebe grabbed the car back off Alyssa and set it up on the track again.

"Good morning," Alyssa said before planting a kiss on my lips. "How are you feeling this morning . . . about everything?"

"I'm fucking fantastic."

She frowned at my swearing but didn't comment on it because Phoebe was too engrossed in her toys to care what I said.

"How are you?" I asked, moving behind her and wrapping my arms around her waist so I could press my hands against her stomach. Before she could answer, I rested my chin on her shoulder and kissed her neck.

The sound that left her went straight to my cock.

"I'm okay. I need to talk to you, though."

A little frown tugged at my brow. "About what?"

"I'm not made of glass." She half-twisted in my hold so she could give me a pointed stare. "There isn't much damage Phoebe can do."

"I don't want her to hurt the—"

She silenced me with a look.

"I don't want you getting hurt."

"It's okay. There's a little bit of padding by a few vital organs before anything can harm . . ." She trailed off. "So it's okay. You don't need to worry about Phoebe accidentally hurting me, okay?"

It went against my better judgement, but I didn't want to argue on Christmas morning.

"Okay." I sealed my agreement with a kiss against the curve of her neck.

A series of little noises left her; they weren't necessarily ones that hinted at enjoyment, but there was a definite bedroom vibe to them.

"What's wrong?" I asked.

"My hormones are driving me crazy," she purred as she pushed her arse back against my cock and her breathing quickened. "It wasn't like this last time."

I rubbed my hands on her stomach, running from just below her breasts down to her pelvis and then back up again. She pushed back harder, and reached around with one hand to cup my arse. "I'm not gonna lie, Lys, I'm pretty fucking glad to hear you weren't so horny around others."

She chuckled, before running her hand along my thigh. "I wish Mum and Dad were coming today," she murmured as she tipped her head back onto my shoulder. "The things I'd do right now if we had some time alone."

The hunger in her eyes when she turned to look at me made it crystal clear what she meant. Fuck. Why did anyone ever complain about their wives getting pregnant? It was making Alyssa rub up and down against me like a dog in heat and I had zero complaints about that at all.

"Hmm, maybe after breakfast we can convince Phoebe to watch an episode or two of *The Wiggles*."

"Wiggles?" Phoebe jumped up. "Can I?"

"Go on then," Alyssa said with a laugh. "You know how to set it up."

The instant Phoebe left the room to go downstairs, Alyssa put her cup down on the bedside table and attacked me. Her hands were in my hair and on my shoulders and running over my boxer shorts.

They never stopped moving.

It was like making out with an octopus, in the best possible way. I couldn't even move my arms to hold her back because she was moving and shifting, rubbing her body against mine as she backed me up to the wall. Her lips were almost punishing as she kissed me. She was a woman possessed. I took it all—everything she was willing to give me.

"Oh God," she murmured against my ear, her breath hot and heavy as she guided my hand into the dip just below her breast. She murmured it again as she ground her pussy against my thigh. Then, just as suddenly as the attack had started, it stopped.

"Oh God!" She moaned as she clamped her hand over her mouth and ran from the room. An instant later, I heard the toilet lid crash against the cistern followed by the sound of retching.

"Lys, are you okay?" I asked, grabbing her tea from Phoebe's bedside table and going in search of her.

I found her in the main bathroom washing her mouth out.

"Are you sure you're happy about this?" she asked.

"About you being sick? Absolutely not. But about the rest . . . Lys, I couldn't be happier. I know I said I didn't want kids, but I was a fucking idiot. I can't wait to meet that little one you've got growing in there." Even as I said the words, it really struck me. She was growing a life. My child.

Holy fuck.

My heart skipped. I'd always thought Alyssa was beautiful. But right in that moment, even with her cleaning up after herself, she was more radiant and powerful than I'd ever seen her. She was a fucking goddess.

My fucking goddess.

"Fuck, I love you," I said.

She chuckled. "Ever the romantic. It's no wonder I fell for you."

"You're really okay?" I tried not to sound worried, but even I heard the concern in my voice.

She offered me a reassuring smile and a nod. "It was a lot worse with the twins. But maybe it would be a good idea to keep that cup away from me."

I left her to go sort out some breakfast for us all. If kissing me made her sick, I could only imagine what the smell of bacon and eggs would do.

When I hit the bottom of the stairs, I was reminded of the dwindling days in our little house.

A year ago, we were in Browns Plains planning her move to be with me in Sydney, and now we were in the midst of our move back to our hometown.

Only this time, we had a shit-ton of my furniture to sell. We'd already arranged with Mum to rent her house since her tenants had moved out a few months earlier and it was sitting vacant. She'd been going around to clean it as often as she could, but had no desire to live there again.

Too many memories, she said.

In just under three weeks, we'd pack up and head home.

Despite saying goodbye to a house at least three times bigger than Mum's, and having to sell the majority of my collection of cars because the cost of shipping them all to Queensland was going to be too high, I was the happiest I'd been in years.

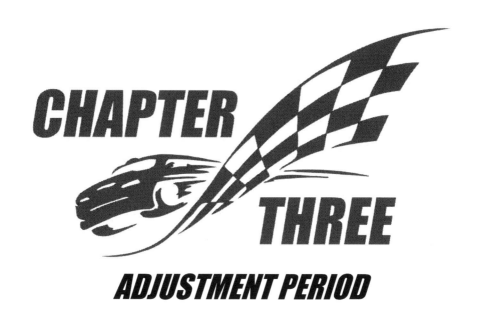

CHAPTER THREE

ADJUSTMENT PERIOD

"I CAN'T BELIEVE this will be our last session together, Doc."

I sat in the tub chair and put my feet up on Dr Henrikson's coffee table—just because I knew it bugged him. If it was going to be our last session, I wanted to make it a memorable one. Christmas and New Year's had come and gone with a visit from Alyssa's family. Despite the slight strain in the air, it wasn't nearly as bad as I'd worried it might have been.

The small breakthroughs I'd had with her father, Curtis, and brother, Josh, over the previous twelve months continued to ease the tension between us all. The fact that Alyssa and I were still happy and together after living together for twelve months in Sydney and were celebrating nearly six months of wedded bliss probably helped too. It probably would've solidified our bonds to tell them about the baby, but Alyssa was dead set on keeping it quiet until after the twelve weeks. Which meant it was easiest just to wait until we got settled in to our new home. We hadn't even told Phoebe yet.

Dr Henrikson's gaze cut to my feet and he raised a brow but didn't say anything. "It doesn't have to be our last session."

"Are you fishing for more money?" I laughed.

He gave a small chuckle. "You know I'll always be available by phone if you need me. And my office will always be open to you should you need it."

"I know, Doc, but honestly, I feel so fucking great. It's not like it was even a few months ago either. It's not like I have to be at Lys's side to feel calm. I just feel like I'm in a good place in my life. I mean, don't get me wrong, I'm shit scared of some of the things I've got coming up. I mean, what the fuck do I know about running a race team? But despite that, I kinda feel like I'll be okay with it all."

He smiled at me in a way that told me he was genuinely happy with the progress I'd made.

"Who would've guessed the little shithead who walked in here five years ago trying to kick his burgeoning ice and weed habit would've been sitting here today ready to face the world as a fucking entrepreneur."

He chuckled. "Well, I did always have hope for you, Declan."

"Except maybe when I flipped out on you." It was almost easy to look back at that time with a laugh. How had I ever thought trying to hide away from my feelings for Alyssa was a good idea?

"Even then. Although, I will admit a part of me worried you'd return to your habits."

I glanced at my hands and frowned. "Do you still worry that?"

He gave me a stern look. "You have an addictive personality, Declan."

"Are you saying you're addicted to me?" I laughed. It was too easy to be laid-back and jokey. "I know I do, and I know I'll have to battle against it forever. But for now, my new addiction is my family. And life. Not just Alyssa, but all of it. The good and the bad."

"I'm glad to hear that. And how is the lovely Alyssa?"

I fought my grin. Because we'd scaled my appointments right back, I hadn't had the opportunity to tell him the good news yet. "She's pregnant."

"Well, that explains the mood," he replied, a grin on his lips. "How are you feeling about that?"

I couldn't fight the smile on my lips, not that I wanted to. "Over the fucking moon." I spent the next little while talking about Alyssa, about her symptoms and our plans. By the end of the session, I was feeling even better than I had going in.

"Keep in touch, won't you, Dec?" He offered me his hand.

"Sure thing."

"And don't forget the tools you have to help with difficult situations."

"Never. Thank you, Doc, for everything." It was a genuine thanks. If it wasn't for him, for his willingness to do phone sessions and his slightly unconventional approach, I don't think I would have survived beyond my first few months at Sinclair. I definitely wouldn't have Alyssa back in my life.

He extended his hand. I stared at it for a beat, thinking about all this man had done for me. A handshake wouldn't cut it as a goodbye. So I hugged him instead.

When I stepped back, Dr Henrikson blinked in surprise, but recovered quickly. "Happy moving."

"Thanks again, Doc."

WHEN I got home, I found Alyssa and Phoebe packing up the last of Phoebe's clothes into a suitcase. I couldn't believe we'd be getting into two cars and driving home in the morning. Alyssa was going to drive my Monaro, and I was taking the Prado with the trailer in tow. It meant those two cars at least could come with me. My Impala and Fairlane—the two cars I was keeping from my collection—were already on their way to Brisbane.

I gave Alyssa a questioning gaze, silently asking her if we were going to tell Phoebe about her baby brother now that we'd had the twelve-week scan and knew that the baby was a healthy little boy. Although it would usually have been a little early to tell for certain, apparently our son liked to show off and gave the doctor a very clear view. I couldn't help my laughter when Alyssa had rolled her eyes and muttered something about him being just like his daddy.

She nodded and smiled. "Phoebe, honey, can you come sit with me and Daddy for a bit?" she asked, patting the bed.

Phoebe grabbed her dolly—the one "Santa" had brought for her—and hopped onto her bed between Alyssa and me.

"You know Mummy and Daddy love you very much, don't you, sweetheart?" Alyssa started.

Phoebe looked at me and Alyssa and nodded. Her smile was so sweet and her cheeks strained with how wide her smile was.

"Well, we've got a little more love coming into our lives soon." Alyssa cupped her cheek.

"What d'you mean?" Phoebe asked.

"Mummy's going to have a baby." I smiled. Alyssa's eyes, full of love, met mine. Reaching behind Phoebe's back, I squeezed Alyssa's hand hoping she knew I was still ecstatic about the news.

"You're going to have a little brother," Alyssa said.

Phoebe nodded but kept playing with her doll. "Will he have to stay in the ground like Emmie?"

My heart stopped and Alyssa gave a half sob. When I glanced at her, I could see the tears building in her eyes. But so much worse was the panic hidden below that. Suffering through what she had with the twins was part of the reason she hadn't wanted more kids.

I stroked my thumb along the back of Alyssa's hand, letting her know that this time would be different.

"No, baby girl," I said. "He'll be able to come and live with us. You'll have to help us take good care of him when he comes home, and help Mummy out as much as you can until then."

"When's he going to come?" Phoebe bit her bottom lip and gazed toward the door expectedly, as though someone was about to come and hand us a baby right then.

"Not for a while yet, honey," Alyssa said, stowing away her tears. "Maybe around your birthday."

"I get a baby brover for my birthday?" Phoebe's eyes lit up.

"We can't promise he'll be here *on* your birthday." Alyssa laughed. "He might come before or after."

"I like babies," Phoebe said. "Like Noah. He was bigger now than last time we saw him, though."

"Babies do that," Alyssa said with a hint of sadness creeping into her voice.. "They grow bigger and bigger until they're all grown up before you realise it."

"When I'm growed up, I want to have lots of babies." Phoebe grabbed her doll and laid it on her arm like she'd been shown to hold Noah.

"How many is lots?" My voice wavered as I raked my hand through my hair. Her innocent words made me think of her growing up. Of boyfriends and the possibility of her heart being broken by some jerk. Of her having a family of her own—of her giving me grandchildren.

"Sweetie, I don't think that's a good idea." Tears fill Alyssa's eyes.

"Why not, Mummy?"

Alyssa blinked repeatedly. Her voice cracked when she said, "Because it might not be safe for you to have babies. Remember we've talked about Emmie's gift, and how it's inside your tummy and you have to take lots of care of it to keep you healthy?"

My stomach twisted at the way Alyssa was speaking. I hadn't witnessed one of the conversations she was talking about, but just the way she said the words chilled my blood.

"I hate Emmie's gift," Phoebe said with a pout. "I can't do anything because of it. Why'd he give it to me?"

"Because you were very, very sick, and it made you better. And if you don't take care of it, you might get very sick again." Alyssa's face became ashen. Her eyes, overly bright with unshed tears, showed me a depth of emotion I was unaware of.

I rubbed my forehead. Wasn't Phoebe out of the woods? Hadn't she gotten Emmanuel's kidney and that'd made her fit and healthy again? Outside of the routine of medications she had to have, and Alyssa's tendency to be overprotective when it came to germs, Phoebe was completely normal. Wasn't she?

"But I wanna have lots of babies to play with," Phoebe whined.

"Maybe you'll be able to." Alyssa rubbed Phoebe's back. "But you need to make sure you speak to your special doctors first, okay? Like we do with everything new."

Phoebe hung her head and muttered, "Yes, Mummy."

She had only had a few specialist appointments during the time they'd lived with me, but Alyssa had generally taken her alone, telling me that it was just a routine visit to check medication levels. Despite that, I'd insisted on going to the first one. It had been exactly what she'd told me about and certainly hadn't gone over new information.

"Lys—" I cleared my throat before continuing, unable to speak around the golf-ball sized swell in my throat. "Can I talk to you a minute?" The words left as I headed for the door, not waiting to see if Alyssa was coming.

"Sure," she said before turning to Phoebe. "Just finish packing your toys into that box like I showed you, okay?"

A moment later, Alyssa was following me.

"What the fuck was that about?" I asked.

"What?" Alyssa's bravery faded and the tears welled in her eyes before slipping down her cheeks. She knew exactly what I was talking about. I lowered my voice. "That shit about telling Phoebe she couldn't have babies."

Her mouth mashed into a hard line as her brow dipped. "I don't want to fill her with false hope."

"What the fuck are you talking about?" I clutched my hair and turned away from her.

Alyssa wiped her eyes, and then blinked at me, as if she couldn't figure me out. Finally, realizing her error, she sighed. "Sometimes it's easy to forget you weren't there for all the warnings."

My heart stopped beating and my blood froze in my veins. "What warnings?"

"Even with a match as good as Emmanuel was, a donated kidney won't last forever."

"What're you saying?" I knew what she was saying, but my mind rejected it.

"Nothing." Alyssa shook her head. "She might be one of the

34

lucky ones."

"But?"

"But the survival rates of a childhood kidney transplant recipient aren't pretty. Things like pregnancy put a strain on the body, especially on the kidneys. It's not impossible, but it's something she should only do with proper monitoring. I'd rather train her to make sensible decisions now than have her do something stupid later."

My mind focused on the words *"survival rates aren't pretty."* How could Alyssa not have told me this sooner?

My throat tightened, making the words difficult to say. "Are you trying to tell me she's going to . . . she'd going to die young?" Fuck, I'd given up Dr Henrikson far too soon. I didn't have enough tools in my emotional toolbox to deal with this information.

As if she could see the betrayal and blame building in me, Alyssa reached her hand out. "I'm sorry, Dec. It's not like I deliberately kept you in the dark. You try to fill her life up so much, like at Easter and Christmas. I figured you'd looked into it and knew."

I swayed and struggled for air. "I just wanted her to be happy. I wasn't making up for anything. How am I supposed to deal with this?"

Alyssa wrapped her arms around my waist. "Just keep living our lives the way we have been, Dec. That's how you deal with it. Because then she'll have the best life she can whether she lives to be twenty or a hundred and two."

Twenty. It struck me in the gut. She could be gone by twenty?

Fuck! Just minutes earlier, I'd imagined Phoebe with boyfriends and a possible family. How the hell was I supposed to deal with the information that I might have to plan her funeral instead of enjoying grandkids?

I drew out of Alyssa's embrace and paced again on shaky legs as my breath grew shorter. There wasn't enough room in the tiny hallway. I could've sworn the walls were closing in tighter. Fuck!

"There's no guarantees in any of this." Alyssa stood in front of me, grabbing my shoulders so she could look in my eyes. Clearly she'd seen my panic and was trying to draw me back from the ledge—just like I had with her fear of going through another pregnancy. "As I said, she might be one of the lucky ones. Us Reedes always have a bit of luck on our side, right?"

Panting, I nodded, willing to let her soothe away the worry with her earnest gaze and gentle caress. She was right. There were no guarantees in life. The way I'd been heading before I found my way back to my family, I could've easily killed myself before I was twenty-five. Fuck knows I'd come close to it often enough. My body shook as I pulled Alyssa into my arms and rubbed my hand over her back as I reminded myself of all the ways her statement was true. The number of accidents that should have killed me. The fact that we had our second chance. I swallowed hard and nodded again, willing to convince myself that everything would be okay. I let the panic sink back to the depths. Stressing wasn't going to help anything.

"Let's just get ready for the move, shall we?" Alyssa grabbed my hand and led me back into Phoebe's room to help her pack.

CHAPTER FOUR

HOME SWEET HOME

.

THE DRIVE FROM Sydney to our new home in Browns Plains—the one that was my parents' old home—took two days in the end.

I'd thought the previous move had taken a long time, what with the regular potty breaks for Phoebe. This time, it wasn't Phoebe's walnut-sized bladder but Alyssa's. Although she blamed the baby, I didn't see how that would be the case. She kept telling me that he was only a few inches long, so I didn't see how such a small thing could cause such an extra need to pee. Still, we stopped almost every hour for Alyssa to pee, and nearly as often for her to be sick.

We spent the night in Coffs Harbour once again. Partly because we'd set off so late after having breakfast with our friends. Eden and Morgan were ecstatic to learn about the baby. The other part was because I didn't like the idea of Alyssa driving alone at night.

"Where's my baby brover now?" Phoebe asked. "Can we get him sooner than my birthday?"

It was clear she'd been digesting the news over the last day and was ready to talk some more about it.

"He's too little at the moment. He needs to grow some more first, so he's somewhere safe and warm where I can look after him," Alyssa said.

Phoebe looked solemn for a moment. "So where is he?"

"He's in Mummy's tummy." Alyssa pulled her sleep shirt tight across her small but growing baby bump. "In there."

Phoebe shifted to lay her head on Alyssa's lap, making Alyssa and me chuckle. After a moment, Phoebe lifted her head. "I can't heared him."

"You won't be able to." Alyssa opened her arms, inviting Phoebe to snuggle closer. At first Alyssa winced—no doubt as Phoebe brushed near Alyssa's sensitive boobs—but then she smiled. "But you'll be able to feel him soon. In a few more weeks, he'll be big enough that you'll be able to feel him kicking."

"Daddy, will you feel that too?"

"I can't wait." I wasn't lying. Since Alyssa had handed me the stick on Christmas Eve announcing pregnancy, I'd wished for something tangible to prove our new baby was alive and well. Alyssa at least got that. Not that I wanted to suffer through the things she had to deal with. Still, feeling something like a kick or a squirm would be more than enough evidence for me. It would be everything—at least until he was born.

I shifted closer to the two of them, curling one hand into Phoebe's hair and resting the other on Alyssa's belly. She rested her hand on the top and grinned at me. For that moment, life was perfect.

OUR PERFECT moment didn't last long. When I woke the next morning, it was to the dulcet tones of Alyssa vomiting in the hotel en suite. I lifted my head to check on her, but my question died on my lips when she heaved again.

"What's wrong with Mummy?" Phoebe asked, her little voice full of concern.

"Your baby brother is making himself known," I said without thinking as I climbed from the bed to see if Alyssa needed anything.

Phoebe was right behind me. "Is he coming now? But he's too little." The panic in her little voice was almost heartbreaking.

I chuckled. "No, sweetie, he's just making Mummy a little sick, that's all."

A pout formed on her lips and a frown creased her brow. "I don't like Mummy being sick. I don't want a brover if it makes Mummy sick."

"It's okay. It's the sort of sick that goes away. It's not that bad."

When the tap in the bathroom shut off with a shudder, my gaze cut to Alyssa. "Not that bad?" she snapped. "How would you like to wake in the morning needing to puke your guts out? To be nauseous. All. The. Time." She yanked the hand towel off the rack and dried her hands before wiping her mouth.

"You know what I meant, Lys." I nodded in Phoebe's direction, trying to let Alyssa know that I'd said what I had in order to stop our daughter from panicking or learning to hate her brother.

"Yeah, sure, I know exactly what you meant." She slammed the towel down on the bathroom counter. "I'm sure it's fantastic that you get to share in the spoils and suffer none of the strain. Story of your life, isn't it?"

I raised my hands in surrender and frowned. "That's not fair."

"No." She narrowed her eyes at me. "What's not fair is me having to go through all of this just because *you* wanted another baby!"

I blinked at her as I processed the words, unable to believe they'd left her. Was she fucking serious? She'd said she was ready to try again. That she wanted to grow our little family too. Had she lied to me? As I was trying to formulate an appropriate response, she started crying.

"What if something goes wrong, Dec?" Alyssa chocked out through her tears.

Phoebe rushed to Alyssa's side and wrapped her arms around Alyssa's thighs.

"Nothing's going to go wrong," I reassured as I crossed the

room to embrace both my girls. I lifted Phoebe onto my hip and the two of us hugged Alyssa.

Once she was safe in my arms, Alyssa's tears fell harder. I didn't say anything—wasn't sure what I could say that wouldn't bring back the rage machine she'd been a few minutes earlier or send her into a fresh round of tears. Slowly, her tears abated to mere sniffles and she held us both in response.

"God, I'm hungry," Alyssa said as she pulled back a moment later and gave Phoebe and me a smile.

My mouth slackened. I found myself speechless. How the hell was I supposed to know how to deal with someone who went through every emotion in less than an hour?

Her anger resurfaced when I asked whether she'd be okay to get back on the road. I really needed to figure out how to not piss her off if I intended on seeing the day our baby was born. If only I knew what it was about the phrase, "Do you reckon you'll be able to handle the Monaro to get home?" that set Alyssa off.

AFTER ANOTHER day of regular stops, slow progress—with regular trips on the mood swing express—we made it to Mum's house.

Our house.

Mum was there to greet us. Phoebe rushed straight to her side and practically threw herself into Mum's arms, who ducked down to catch her before standing upright again.

"Guess what, Nana," she said with a grin that stretched from ear to ear.

"What?"

"I'm getting a baby brover for my birthday."

My heart pounded in my chest. Alyssa and I had discussed the possibility of telling family—we were past the danger zone after all—but hadn't firmly decided on when, or who to tell first. I worried Phoebe's slip might bring out the Hulk temporarily living inside my wife once more.

"What?" Mum's gaze shifted from Phoebe to me. I couldn't hide the shit-eating grin on my lips. Before she said anything more, her gaze cut to Alyssa's stomach and the barely there bump beneath her dress. I could see the moment the when truth hit her and she lit up. "Wow. That's exciting isn't it?" she asked Phoebe.

"He's not a very nice brover, though." Phoebe stuck her bottom lip out.

Mum raised one brow and her gaze fell to me, suspicion clear in her eyes. "Why do you say that?"

I swallowed as I waited for Phoebe's response, although I was certain I could guess what it was.

"'Cause he makes Mummy very sick, and that's not nice."

Mum chuckled. "When your daddy was a baby he made me very sick too. That's just what babies do. Not because they're mean, but because they can't help it."

Phoebe tilted her head to the side and frowned, deep in thought. Finally, she smiled and nodded.

"Did you want to see your room?" Mum asked as she put Phoebe on the ground. When Phoebe nodded, Mum added, "It's the one at the end of the hallway. I'll be down in a minute."

Phoebe rushed into the house and Mum covered the ground back to Alyssa and me.

"Wow, congratulations, you two," she said. Her tone belied the joy she felt. I was certain she believed Phoebe and Emmanuel would be her only grandchildren. "I can't believe I'm going to be a nana again."

"Thank you," Alyssa said with a smile. She practically radiated with contentment. Fuck, she was gorgeous. "No one else knows yet though, so can you keep it on the down-low for now? Just until we get to see Mum and Dad on the weekend."

"Of course," Mum said, bringing Alyssa into her arms. "Congratulations," she said again. Her smile was so bright, so wide, it was easy to believe she was the one who was pregnant. She added almost silently, "And thank you."

After she'd hugged Alyssa, Mum came to me while Alyssa trailed into the house—no doubt trying to ensure Phoebe wasn't getting up to any mischief. Her eyes were so bright, and the smile that still graced her lips took at least ten years off her appearance. She didn't even have to ask before I wrapped my arms around her.

For a while, our relationship had been strained—almost fractured—but it was stronger than ever. When she'd returned from her extended overseas holiday, she started getting out more and more. She even had a close circle of friends in the city. She didn't mind telling everyone her newfound confidence was all because of me. I'd given her the permission she'd needed to leave Dad.

"Are you happy about the baby?" she whispered as she glanced across at Alyssa.

Did she think I was pushed into it? That I didn't want more children? "Happy? Mum, I'm over the fucking moon. I can't believe I'm lucky enough to get to experience it all with Lys from the beginning this time."

She squeezed my arm reassuringly. "Take care of her." Her smile fell, no doubt as ghosts of the past haunted her memories. "It's not going to be an easy journey for her after the outcome last time."

I nodded. "I'm definitely trying. Although it'd be easier if there was an instruction manual."

Her laugh was easy and carefree; it was pretty damn good to hear. "I don't think there's a husband out there who doesn't wish for one of those. Just remember, there's not much trouble silence can get you into. Unless she's asked a question about how she looks, in which case you need a fast and appropriate yes or no, or there'll be hell to pay. Better yet, just tell her how beautiful she is."

"What was it like for her, last time I mean?" It was something I'd wanted to ask, but didn't know how to raise it with Alyssa. I was certain she'd downplay the worst parts, but Mum would give it to me straight.

"She had it pretty rough. Morning sickness most of the way, mood swings like you couldn't believe, and the appetite of a small hippo. Mind you, I think that last one might have been because she'd neglected herself so much in the first couple of months."

My stomach fell when I realised I was the reason she'd

neglected herself. It was what her father had mentioned during our wedding. *You're a fucking idiot, Reede.*

"Don't worry too much about it, honey. I guarantee all she'll need is for you to be there for her. Just try not to take anything she says to heart."

I recalled her accusation that morning. Don't take it personal. Easier said than done. Surely it couldn't get much worse, could it?

CHAPTER FIVE

SWING SWING

AFTER TELLING ALYSSA'S family about the pregnancy, I was treated to the expected round of excited squeals from Alyssa; her mother, Ruth; and sister-in-law, Ruby. Curtis and Josh were more subdued but still offered congratulatory handshakes to me and hugs to Alyssa. Phoebe took great delight in the attention lavished on her about the fact that she was going to be a big sister.

As we were about to leave, Ruth pulled Alyssa aside, and they had a brief, private conversation that looked more heated than most of theirs usually got. Alyssa's lips pressed together as she shot me an accusatory look and then disappeared down the hallway with her mum. When they returned, Ruth was carrying a box and Alyssa had an oversized satchel bag stuffed full of something.

Understanding that I was required to be a packhorse for a moment, I grabbed the bag off Alyssa and the box from Ruth. I didn't ask what was in there—obviously that was a source of contention between the two of them—but I played the part of the dutiful husband so I didn't get chewed out later on for being an arsehole, or whatever insult Alyssa could come up with for me.

The instant we were in the car, Alyssa blew up. "How dare she do that!"

I wasn't sure if it was safe to ask who or what she was talking about. In the end, I figured it was the safer bet. The other option could make Alyssa think I didn't care.

"How dare who do what?"

She hit the air in front of her. "Mum. How dare she keep all the stuff I told her to throw out!"

"I'm lost," I admitted.

Alyssa pinched the bridge of her nose and sighed. "I moved out of home not long after Phoebe was a year old. I needed my own space, and we needed to be a family. Mum asked me what I wanted her to do with the baby stuff, and I told her to throw it all out because I wasn't going through that again. She didn't. She kept it all. Including the cot, the change table, everything. Ruby's got those for the moment, but apparently by the time this one is born, we'll be able to have them back."

I failed to see what the problem was but didn't want to say that. I was almost positive that speaking those words out loud would be enough to see me castrated while I slept that night. Taking a breath, I searched for the least offensive way to say what was needed. "It's a blessing in disguise though, isn't it?"

She growled at me. "Of course, I can't expect *you* to understand. I wasn't having more kids, Dec. I told her that. I told her to get rid of it all because I would never need it again, and she didn't."

"But you do—" I cut off when I saw the gaze she turned on me. The honey brown in her eyes was like liquid gold, swirling and leaping out in molten fire. It wasn't going to help anyone arguing with her that she did, in fact, need the items because she was in fact having more kids. She obviously wasn't in the mood to hear it.

"That's not the point, Dec. The point is that she blatantly disregarded what I asked her to do. She ignored what I wanted. And then she loaned out my cot and change table when they weren't even hers to give."

My fingers tightened around the steering wheel as I tried not to voice the things spinning in my mind. If she didn't want the fucking stuff, she could hardly be upset that someone else was using it, could she?

Risking another quick glance at her out of the corner of my eye, I saw that the answer was yes. Yes, she absolutely could. How the fuck was I going to make it another six months dealing with the confusing logic presented by pregnant Alyssa?

I just hoped like fuck that there were no old articles or newspapers lying around to remind her of the way my life had been after I'd left home and before I found my way back to her again. Something told me any reminders of trysts with anyone else would end badly for me.

AFTER PHOEBE was asleep, I grabbed the box and bag that Ruth had given to Alyssa from the car. When I put it on the coffee table, Alyssa scowled at me. "Some of it might come in handy," I argued at the risk of facing her ire.

On the top of the box was a strange-looking device. It looked a little like a miniature bullhorn, with a bottle attached to the bottom. When I lifted it, my finger squeezed the trigger. A wheezing intake and the creak of a spring accompanied the action. Even though I wanted to drop it again straight away, I let the machine hang off my index finger instead. "What the fuck is this shit?"

Alyssa laughed and reached out for the torture implement. "It's a breast pump."

"To do what?"

"Express milk. For when I can't be near the baby."

I curled my nose in disgust as I dropped it into her palm. "So what . . . you milk yourself? Like a cow?"

"Yes," the irritation in her tone was clear, "exactly like a fucking cow. Because that's what this pregnancy will make me. A fat cow."

My eyes widened as I saw the minefield laid out in front of me. Goddamn, it was going to be difficult to traverse this one. The problem was, I was already deep in the field and there was no easy way to back out. Worse, one toe was pressing against the pressure plate, and if I wasn't fucking careful, the whole thing would blow up in my face. I couldn't say she wouldn't get fat because I didn't fucking know. Maybe the pregnancy would make her six times the size she was, but I did know I'd love her still. Sure she had a banging body, but that wasn't what I loved about her.

Of course, I couldn't say that I'd love her whatever size she was because she'd immediately think I was trying to cover up for the fact that she was already a few kilos heavier—not that I thought she was, but *she* thought she was. Her logic was based on the simple fact that it was harder to do up her jeans—hence the dresses—but I didn't see how that was proof she'd put on any weight other than the baby bump, which would naturally be in the way of jeans.

If I tried to tell her she was beautiful, I'd get in trouble for only caring about her looks.

I did the only thing I could think of in the situation. I grabbed the pump off her and dropped it back into the box before pressing my lips against hers. When our lips touched, I kissed her harder than I had since the morning after Christmas when my kisses induced a vomiting spell—hardly a confidence booster.

Despite the shock in her body, she responded almost immediately to my kiss, twisting her tongue around mine in sexy little motions. My hands roamed her body, but when I tried to palm her breast, she smacked my hand out of the way. I took the hint and moved on to her arse instead, before drawing her legs up around my waist.

Leaving the boxes full of shit for baby behind us, I carried her to the bedroom.

"What are you doing?" Alyssa asked with a laugh.

"I'm taking my wife to our bedroom and fucking her good and proper."

Her eyes pinched at the edges. "Does your wife get a say in this?"

"Are you saying no?" I went to drop her back to the floor.

She locked her legs around my waist. "No."

"So you're saying yes?"

She chuckled. "Yes."

"Good, because I fucking need you, Lys." It might have started as a way of distracting her from the crap going on in the living room, but it quickly escalated into a genuine need.

Sitting her on the edge of the bed, I stripped her dress off in one swift motion before claiming her skin all over with my lips. Relishing the attention, she relaxed back onto the mattress, leaving the little swell between her hips on full display.

Fuck, she was so goddamned beautiful.

I dropped to my knees in front of her and kissed the bump. Her twisted in my hair, brushing through the soft spikes.

"We did this, Lys," I murmured against the small protrusion before slowly drawing her panties off.

"Fuck," she growled as she watched me move.

With our gazes locked, I kissed up her leg—starting at her knee and trailing up her inner thigh. She licked her lips in anticipation as I neared the sweet spot at the apex of her thighs. Fuck, I needed to taste her pussy again; it'd been too long. Then again, a few hours was too long when it came to Alyssa.

Without breaking our eye contact, I teased her open with my fingers and ran my tongue across her lower lips in one long, smooth trail. The sweet and tangy taste of her made me groan as my eyes sank closed.

"Fuck, Lys," I murmured before grabbing her legs and yanking her pussy closer to my mouth. I had no time for gentle. No need for slow. I wanted her panting and screaming my name, and I wanted it now.

After I'd tipped her over the edge with my mouth and fingers, she took control and guided me onto the bed. She'd stripped me in record time before climbing on top to ride me. With the new angle, I could see the pregnancy hadn't just swelled her belly. Her boobs were at least half a cup bigger than the last time she'd been above me.

So fucking sexy.

We spent the rest of the night wrapped up together. No matter how many times I made Alyssa scream my name as she came, it wasn't enough for her.

I woke the next morning with her arse wiggling back against my morning wood.

"Are you trying to fucking wear it out?" I asked with a chuckle.

"What do you mean?" she mumbled sleepily as she pushed back again.

I grabbed her hips to press them firmly against my hard-on so that at least it wasn't at the mercy of Alyssa's relentless wriggling. "I mean that I counted at least six orgasms last night, and you're ready for more."

"What can I say?" Her tone teased as she reached back to dig her nails into my hip. "You make me insatiable."

"Never like this though," I murmured against her neck. "You're going to give me cock burn."

She spun in my hold and lifted her brow. "Are you saying my sexual appetite is too big for the great Declan Reede, ladies' man extraordinaire?"

I heard the challenge in her tone and was determined to answer it. "Oh, that's it!" I growled as I pounced on her, flipping our bodies so I was on top. "Now you're in trouble."

"That's good," she purred as she stretched out beneath me. "I love trouble!"

I was sure I had one more round in me, and if that wasn't enough, we'd just have to have a visit from the vibrating friend she'd taken with her to London.

I had no idea how I was going to get through the next six-ish months with her mood swings and needs, but I was determined to do it the best way I could. And I'd fight anything to make her happy—even a mild case of friction burn.

CHAPTER SIX

VEEBACK

THE FIRST FEW weeks in our new home and life went far too fast. It was all a blur of revealing the new graphics for our team cars. All the Wood Racing livery had been stripped over the silly season and changed to our Emmanuel Racing design. The name change was something Paige had resisted but ultimately had to suck up and accept. She didn't even have a say in the graphics. Her side of the sale agreement might have stretched to consulting and a profit share, but Alyssa and I were responsible for all the major decisions. We settled on a rearing horse leading the name, Emmanuel Racing, and colours that matched those on my custom helmet.

The only day Alyssa and I had off during those crazy weeks was Phoebe's first day at school. We were both there to meet her teacher and introduce her to the school community. Eventually the plan was for Alyssa to work from home, around school hours, to be there for Phoebe and the baby.

In the short term though, Mum was taking up that responsibility around the part-time cleaning business she'd started.

Although we wanted to settle into the eventual routine sooner rather than later, there was just too much we needed to get sorted. And we'd only had a very short time to do it because a week after Phoebe started school I was on my way to Yas for the first round of the season.

Thankfully there were only two overseas races in the season, and the other was in New Zealand. It meant there wasn't the almost month-long stay away from home that there had been the year before.

When I lined up for qualifying in the Yas race, I buzzed with nervous energy. It was the first race with me in complete and sole control of the car I now financed—the business we'd sunk our life savings into. Any crash I was involved in was a hit straight to our profit. Between the bank funding, the share for Paige, and Danny's keen eye on his investment, we needed to keep a tight hold on the purse strings or Emmanuel would be sunk before it even started.

Despite the need for caution, a definite excitement ran through my veins. I could barely keep my enthusiasm in check when I had to go to the owners' meetings and the drivers' meetings. Throughout the lead-up in Yas, I'd caught up with lots of people, including my former pit-crew buddies, met with Danny for some planning meetings, and had lunch with Morgan and Eden McGuire and Dane Kent—who would always be good friends despite being on my former team and technically my rivals.

After qualifying cleanly in midpack, I celebrated in the form of a Skype date with Alyssa and Phoebe.

The weekend was a bit of a torture test because watching Eden getting around with her own growing belly made me think of Alyssa back at home. Their due dates were only weeks apart, with Eden due late May and Alyssa due mid-June.

By the end of the weekend, Emmanuel Racing was on the lips of most of the reporters. We hadn't won a race, but two seconds was enough to take the event because neither of the two first-place winners placed high enough in their other race to beat my combined tally. The number of times I'd uttered the phrase, "Consistency is the key," as I'd been interviewed made the words almost meaningless, but that was going to be our race strategy for the year.

It was only after the event was over that I realised how much more there was to being an owner than to just being a driver. While Morgan, Dane, and the other boys all went back to their hotels to get ready for the flight home, I had to be on hand for all the logistics, arrangements, and final sign-offs on everything. I had good people I was beginning to trust, but there was still so much I had to learn.

"Congratulations on your success this weekend." Danny gave me a grin that told me he didn't mind that Sinclair Racing was behind Emmanuel in the championship. I was sure the order would chop and change a fair bit over the course of the year, but for now, I was happy to accept the glory.

"Not too bad for a rookie, hey?" I flashed him one of my trademark cocky grins. The sort that the sponsors lapped up.

He chuckled. "I learned a long time ago what you can do as a rookie, so I never expected anything less."

His words surprised me, given where we were just over twelve months earlier, but I was glad for them anyway. "Thank you. Having a good mentor helps."

"Not to mention a good woman at your side."

"How can I argue there?" I wasn't sure if it was a bit of a dig at me. Still, I couldn't help but agree with him. Me with Alyssa beside me was better than me without her. I couldn't imagine the way things could have gone without her and Phoebe—the way things were just eighteen months earlier.

"Hazel and I will have to do lunch with you two when we're in Brisbane next."

I never thought I'd be the "doing lunch" type, but as a business owner, I was going to have to get used to it. "We'd like that."

I resisted the urge to let fly with a, "Have your people call my people," but I had some fucking standards and no real people . . . yet.

NOT LONG after I was back from Yas, but before I really had to get ready for the next two races on back-to-back weekends in March, it was time for Alyssa's twenty-week scan and first obstetrician appointment.

I was like a child on Christmas Eve as we waited for the scan. Alyssa, on the other hand, was bouncing off the walls for different reasons.

"Fuck, I need to pee!" she announced for the tenth time since we sat in the waiting room. "Why do they make you drink so much water before these things? It's like they just ignore the fact that there's a baby ready to bounce on it at any second."

"I'm sure they'll be out in a minute, and we'll be done soon."

"They better, Dec, or I'm just going to go to the toilet and they can get screwed. I can't hold this in any longer." Her legs bounced a fast rhythm as she did her own slightly subdued version of a potty dance.

I grabbed her hand. "They'll be out in a minute."

And if they weren't, I'd have some choice words for them for making Alyssa wait.

It was barely five minutes later that the sonographer found us in the waiting room.

"Oh thank Christ for that!" Alyssa snapped as they called her name.

We followed the woman back to the ultrasound room where she guided Alyssa onto the bed. Alyssa pulled her dress up so it was bunched under her boobs and the sonographer tucked paper around it and into Alyssa's panties. It reminded me of our first scan, except this time I wasn't shitting myself quite as much. At least I knew what to expect this time.

Even though I'd seen the evidence of the growing baby—Alyssa's expanding stomach—day by day, it was only seeing that image and contrasting it to the memory of the last scan that made me realise just how big Alyssa was getting. The baby was higher, the bump more rounded than before.

"Are you ready to see your baby?"

The sonographer shifted the screen so Alyssa and I could both see our baby as I sat at Alyssa's side with her hand in mine.

"Let's see what we've got." She pushed the wand against Alyssa's stomach and a mess of black and white moved over the screen. Just like last time, I had no idea what was what until the sonographer pointed it all out. Once she'd pointed out the head, I was able to track that.

"Everything's looking good here," she said as she continued to stop the image every so often for various measurements. "Now, let's get the heartbeat."

Just like the last time, I wasn't in any way prepared for the depth of emotions that welled inside me at the noise. My throat closed and my own heart rushed as the fast whoosh-whoosh sound filled the air accompanied by spikes on the screen. My smile fought through as I glanced at Alyssa, who had tears welling in her eyes.

"Have you guys thought about whether you want to find out the sex?"

Alyssa giggled. "Unless anything's changed, or the last guy got it wrong, we already know."

"Shall we double-check, just to be on the safe side?"

I nodded, and Alyssa said, "Sure."

The last thing we needed was to have promised Phoebe a brother and deliver a sister. Not that I thought she'd mind a sister, but it was best to prepare her.

The sonographer moved the wand around for a moment and pointed out what she was seeing. "This here"—she guided her pointer over the screen—"would suggest you're having a little boy."

Even though it was what we'd been told, it was nice to have the confirmation.

"Ah!" Alyssa sat up, no doubt copping another kick to her liver or something. I felt a stab of jealousy. Even though an internal beating wasn't exactly anyone's idea of fun, it was a connection Alyssa had to the baby that I didn't.

"He's an active little thing." The sonographer laughed. "And he's got a good kick on him."

My gaze shot to her. "What? You felt it?"

With a quiet laugh, she hung up the wand and wiped Alyssa's

belly down with a tissue. Then she reached for my hand. She guided it to the place where the wand had been a moment earlier. "Just . . ." She trailed off and paused for a moment. "There."

Under my palm, Alyssa's stomach flinched. I glanced between the sonographer and Alyssa, who nodded, as if to answer a question I hadn't asked. Maybe my expression belied my confusion over the little nudge. *That* was a kick? That tiny little flinch? I'd felt something similar once or twice over the last week, but I didn't think it was . . .

It hit me.

Holy fuck! They were kicks—I'd felt our baby kick. I wanted to rest both my hands on Alyssa's belly and wait until he moved again—to absorb every motion I could.

"Are you finished?" Alyssa asked, her tone tinged with impatience. At first I thought it might have been directed at me, but she wasn't looking at me.

The sonographer gave a knowing smile. "I'm done. The toilet's through there."

"Thank goodness," Alyssa said before turning her gaze to me. "Can I . . .?"

I realised my hand was still pressed against her stomach and reluctantly tugged it away with an apology on my lips.

"Here you go," the sonographer said, handing me a couple of small sheets of paper. When I glanced down, I saw they were printouts of the baby. My chest tightened as I thought the words again. *Our baby*.

It was still a little surreal, but fucking awesome all at once.

When Alyssa came back into the room—back to her smiling self now that she wasn't battling with a full bladder and active baby— the sonographer gave her a grin. "The reports will go to the maternity ward, but everything looks good."

"Thank you." Alyssa took my hand and led me out.

We had a few hours to kill before our first appointment with the obstetrician, so we went for a little walk to get some food. We soon found ourselves at a burger joint nearby.

Ignoring the last of her food, Alyssa leaned across the table to draw my hands into hers. With her wide eyes and teasing smile, she proved that her words were an understatement. "It's actually nice having some time with you like this."

I didn't need to ask what she meant, because our lives had been crazy and we'd barely had time together alone, let alone enough to stop and share a meal. "It'll get easier, won't it?"

"I hope so, but who knows? I mean when this little one comes, we'll be back to the routine of sleepless nights, nappies, round-the-clock breastfeeding. It's going to be crazy."

I clasped her hands in mine. "I like our kind of crazy."

She sighed and then started to cry. "I do too."

I swiped her tears with my thumb. "These don't suggest you do."

"It's just so much." Her voice cracked. "There are days where I just can't believe what we've become. Where we are. I mean, two years ago . . ."

She was alone and every aspect of my life was sliding down the shitter faster than I would have believed possible when I'd signed my initial contract with Sinclair Racing and left home.

Alyssa sighed and shook her head dreamily. "I was supposed to be on my way to a high-flying law career."

How she'd hated that job. What would our life be like if she still had to face it every day?

I rubbed my thumb over hers. "And I was supposed to be nothing more than a driver. Things change. People change."

Her gaze dropped to our joined hands. "I know."

Leaning further across the table, I cupped her cheek. "Are you happy?" Although I didn't think the question was completely necessary, the fact that she was crying made me ask it.

"I'm ecstatic. I really am. I just keep waiting for the other shoe to drop."

"Lys," I whispered as I leant across the table conspiratorially.

She leant forward too.

"I threw the other fucking shoe away." I gave her my trademark smirk.

A sweet little laugh escaped her. "I love you, Dec."

"I love you too, Lys." I kissed her lips. "We should probably get back to the hospital for the maternity clinic appointment, though."

It was almost an hour and a half later before we were in the doctor's office for our visit. She spoke about various things to Alyssa, but I was only half paying attention. There were some things I didn't want to know about, not even when it came to my wife.

When they started to talk birth plans, my ears pricked up. I needed to know both Alyssa and the baby would be safe. That was my one goal, the one thing I could try to impact.

"I'm interested in a VBAC," Alyssa said.

I screwed my nose up at the word. What the fuck was a veeback? It was the first time I'd heard her talk about anything.

"You understand that can be quite risky?" the doctor said.

"So can a secondary C-section," Alyssa shot back just as quickly. "I can assure you, I'm not coming into this doe-eyed and innocent. I'm all too well aware of the risks of childbirth, both to mother and baby. My caesarean was over five years ago. My scar tissue is well healed. I'm young, fit, and healthy. The reason for my previous caesarean is documented in my file, and if the same thing happens in pregnancy, of course I'll do whatever is necessary to keep both the baby and myself safe. But I've researched the pros and cons of both, and I'd like to try. I think there would be a benefit in VBAC in my circumstances."

"Risks?" I asked as my stomach fell. What did she mean risks? I looked to Alyssa for reassurance, but she wouldn't meet my eye. Did she know this?

My heart raced and all I could hear was a siren going off in my head, warning me that the baby and Alyssa could be in danger.

"Multiple risks," the doctor said. "The most concerning being the risk of uterine rupture."

Rupture wasn't a good word. I didn't like the sound of that risk at all. Especially not concerning Alyssa or the baby.

Alyssa reached for my hand and gave it a gentle squeeze. "There are risks involved with every pregnancy. If I have another C-section, there are risks too. The recovery time will be less if I can have a VBAC. I really would prefer to avoid surgery if I can."

My mind was still spinning around with the words I didn't like and those I didn't understand. I wanted to hold my hand up and say slow the fuck down, but the doc and Alyssa seemed content to continue their conversation.

"Are you considering more children?"

Alyssa turned her gaze to me with the question burning in her eyes.

"Can't we get through this one first?" I asked. I wasn't sure I could take the idea of risks and ruptures all over again. If I'd heard those words before we started trying for a baby, I probably would've refused. My little family of three would have been more than enough if having more kids was going to put Alyssa in danger.

"We can certainly assess your viability as a candidate for trialling a VBAC, especially as you seem willing to consider other options if there's an emergency."

"Can I just ask one question?" My mind still spun with questions and concern for the apparent danger. "What the fuck is veeback?"

Alyssa shook her head and gave a throaty laugh. "Vaginal Birth After Caesarean. It means trying to have a baby naturally even though I had a C-section last time."

I stared at her. I was seriously in over my fucking head with this shit. Worries and thoughts of Alyssa breastfeeding—and pumping her breast milk—of her having to choose between squeezing a child out of her pussy or having surgery, and of what we would do once the baby was born all spun around and around in my head and I started to feel a little light-headed.

"It's too late to back out now, isn't it?" I asked as I climbed to my feet. The walls were closing in on me and I had to escape. My breath grew shorter and shorter and I couldn't get the oxygen I needed. *Holy fuck.*

My eyes rolled up and a bitter, metallic sensation burned the back of my tongue. A second later, Alyssa's hands clasped my cheeks. "Five things you can see."

I blinked as I tried to work out what her words meant. My

lungs were still three sizes too small, my heart at least two too big.

"Five things, Dec," she repeated. Realisation dawned that she was trying to get me to do a grounding exercise that Dr Henrikson had taught us.

"You. The chair. You. The desk. You."

She breathed a sigh of relief, no doubt recalling my statement in that session; I didn't need grounding tools. I just needed her.

"Do you want the four things I can touch?" I asked as my lips twisted into a grin.

Her lips slid into a knowing smile. "No, because I'm sure they're not appropriate to discuss in front of our doctor."

"She's a specialist in at least one of them," I whispered into Alyssa's ear.

She chuckled as she playfully smacked my chest. "And you won't be touching any of them if you don't sit back in that chair."

"Mmm, as if you could resist me, Mrs Insatiable." Her hormone-induced sex-craziness had died down a little—thankfully at a point before she'd killed my cock from overuse—but she was still almost always ready for some fun. Instead of waiting for a reply, I found my way back to the chair.

"I'm sorry," I said to the doctor. "I just got a little overwhelmed for a moment there."

"There isn't much I haven't seen in this office." The humour in her tone proved the truth in her statement. "A first-time father freaking out is hardly the worst of them."

I was going to argue that I wasn't first time—I had a daughter at home after all—but then stopped because she was right. At least in the respect of going through pregnancy, birth, and babies, I was as wet behind the ears as anyone.

"If you'd been through this before, you'd have known the risks involved in every pregnancy," the doctor added, answering the question I didn't ask.

She offered Alyssa a sympathetic look, no doubt thinking that she was a young mother having two pregnancies to two different fathers. The selfish part of me wanted to leave the assumption alone because it meant I didn't have to admit how badly I'd fucked up.

"I was, uh, *absent* during our first pregnancy," I admitted. "A mistake I don't intend to make twice."

Alyssa clasped my hand and intertwined her fingers with mine. The rest of the appointment went smoothly and before long, Alyssa had been given a list of instructions and an idea of her schedule for going back into the antenatal clinic. I was determined to go to as many appointments as I could—and not pass out like a fucking pansy at a single one..

CHAPTER SEVEN

RUSH RUSH

THE END OF March and all through April was nothing short of madness.

I missed every one of Alyssa's appointments because I was overseas or interstate. The race schedule would have been intense enough without having to worry about keeping the team ticking over on top of it all. I was just thankful we'd kept Paige on to handle the bulk of it. I probably could have muddled through, but her advice turned out to be pretty invaluable most of the time.

It seemed every time I stopped, Alyssa's stomach had swollen another couple of inches. I hated that I was missing it all, but if I stopped and jumped off the crazy train, Emmanuel Racing could fail. As it was, because of my distraction every time I hit the track, I'd had one DNF in the eight races, and was coming third in the championship. Still, our times and positions were respectable enough to keep the sponsors happy. I just had to keep it up, even though there were some days I was just about ready to fall in a heap.

The one thing that kept me going without too many complaints was the knowledge that Alyssa's days were almost as busy as mine, and she had the added pressure of growing a human inside her—so really I had no fucking right to complain about anything.

One Friday in the middle of April, I stood in our kitchen and watched as Phoebe shovelled down her Weet-Bix and Alyssa packed everyone's lunches. Even though the Easter long weekend was coming at the end of April, that wouldn't give us a chance to ease the strain because that signalled the start of the school holidays, which meant we needed someone home constantly to watch Phoebe, and there was a race in Perth the following weekend so I'd be up to my eyeballs with work.

Phoebe finished her breakfast and raced to the sink with her dirty bowl. Alyssa twisted around and grabbed Phoebe's bag to put her lunch box inside. It was a familiar dance to us now, one we'd been performing every morning. Some mornings it was a quickstep, other times a slower waltz, but always leading to the moment we split into three different directions. What I wouldn't give for just a couple of days for the three of us to spend some time together before it got even crazier with a new baby in the mix.

"Stop," I said, wishing I could pause the world for a while.

"What?" Alyssa asked as she shoved my insulated lunch bag into my hand.

"Stop," I said a little louder. "Let's just get away."

She paused in front of me. "What are you talking about?"

"Let's just take the day off and get away. Like we did before I went back to work. Just the three of us."

"We can't, we've got—"

"Nothing on that can't wait one more day. I need this, Lys. I need you, and I need Phoebe, and I need to just get away," I pleaded. "Let's go for a drive out to Mount Tamborine for a picnic."

"I don't—"

Moving closer to her, I traced her cheek with my fingertips. "Give me one reason."

"Phoebe's got school."

I lifted my brow at her. "She's in prep. It's not exactly going to impact on her choice of university is it?"

"I guess not."

"C'mon," I said, dragging her closer to me. "Just one day without the team, or school, or anything else. You'd like that, wouldn't you, Pheebs?" I glanced around Alyssa to where Phoebe was standing listening to us.

Phoebe nodded. "Can we go to a playground?"

"We'll find the best playground there is."

She gave an excited giggle.

"But only if Mummy agrees to have the day off."

"Please, Mummy?" Phoebe said, dancing around Alyssa's legs.

"You're playing dirty," Alyssa muttered in my ear.

"I'll play as dirty as I need for the chance for some time alone with my girls."

She narrowed her eyes at me and offered me a sly smile. "You're calling the school and telling them that she's not coming in."

"Deal. But who'll call in for me," I joked. I wondered if she was remembering high school like I was. Back then, we used to wag somewhat regularly and she'd never complained about the way we'd spent the day. Of course, we didn't have a car or the funds to go where we wanted then.

"Uh-uh," Alyssa said, reaching into my pocket and pulling out my phone. "If you wanna ditch, you've gotta dial."

"I'm sure I can be a big boy and do that. I mean, my boss is pretty fantastic, and I'm sure he won't have any complaints when I tell him that I need time with you." I stepped closer to her. "I think he has a crush on you. In fact, I think he wants to fuck you." I whispered in her ear so Phoebe couldn't hear.

She gave my chest a playful shove. "You might work for yourself, but you still have people expecting you in, and you need to let them know you won't be there. And that I won't be available either."

"Will do. You go get yourself and Phoebe ready for some fun, and I'll make the calls."

I jumped on the phone, first with Mum, then with Emmanuel

Racing, and finally with Phoebe's school. Within an hour, we were on the road for a day of absolutely fucking nothing, and I hadn't looked forward to anything more in a while. During the course of the day, we settled on a name for the baby: Brock Curtis, the first name after a racing legend and the second after Alyssa's father.

APRIL ENDED and May came racing around the corner. A few days before I had to leave home for the Winton race, I had an early morning phone call from a very stunned and sleepy-sounding Morgan.

"Is this *the call*?" I asked. I was unable to hide the excitement bubbling in my voice.

"Yeah, it is," he said. The more he talked, the more shell-shocked he sounded. "It's a boy."

Alyssa nudged me to find out what he was saying and then grinned when I nodded.

"Give me a minute; I'll put you on speaker. Lys wants to talk too." I set the phone to speaker.

"Give us all the details," Alyssa said. "How's Eden? How's the baby? Have you picked a name? What was—" She kept rolling off questions until I pressed my finger to her lips.

"Give the man a chance to answer a couple of those questions before asking more." I teased but sobered when she narrowed her eyes at me. Although the worst of her hormonal swings had settled sometime around month five, they'd started up again recently as we hit the last month of her pregnancy.

"He was born three hours ago. His name is Max. He was 3.4 kilos, fifty-one centimetres long, and both mum and bub are doing great."

"Is Eden there?" Alyssa asked. "Can I talk to her?"

"Sorry, Lys, she's rest—" He cut off with a laugh. "Actually she's right here."

Alyssa grabbed the phone off me. "How'd it all go?" The words left her as she walked away with my phone in her hand. I was certain she needed the reassurance about Eden's labour. The closer Alyssa's due date got, the more she panicked. No amount of calming words from me could help. If Eden could help ease her fears, I was happy to let the two of them shoot the shit for as long as they wanted.

Alyssa's voice grew quieter as she headed into the kitchen. I left her to it and figured I'd just have to catch up with Morgan at Winton.

CHAPTER EIGHT

HURRY HOME

BEFORE I KNEW it, June had arrived and Alyssa's due date was barrelling closer. Alyssa was more on edge than ever before when she reached the point where Phoebe's placenta had detached, causing the emergency caesarean for the twins. Still, she was calmer than I expected her to be—and a little fuller than I'd imagined. There was nothing I loved more than to trail my hands over her belly and feel the movements of the life within. It was fucking magical. She was also a little more forgetful and absent-minded than before, but I'd been told that was normal under the circumstances.

With every day, my excitement grew because I couldn't wait for Alyssa's due date so I could meet my newest son.

Between races at the Winton event, Morgan and I had been able to catch up and he'd shown me 1,001 photos of Max. Every possible angle had been captured at least twice. It was sweet to see the photos at first, but by the end, I was fucking relieved it was over. Of course, I didn't say that to him. Instead, I just smiled and nodded as my eyes glazed over after the first ten photos. I figured payback would be a bitch once Brock was born.

Because the Darwin race was on Phoebe's birthday, we debated having the team skip it, but we were still clinging in the top five of the championship and missing the whole event would sink my chances to nonreturnable depths. Plus, Alyssa's due date was the same weekend as the Townsville race, and there was the strong possibility of me having to miss that one regardless. If we missed too many, the sponsors would likely call in track time clauses on their contracts and we'd be up for the penalties. We couldn't afford that.

Instead, we had a dinner for Phoebe's birthday the night before I left, inviting everyone to the party—all of Alyssa's family, my mum, and Flynn.

After the dinner, as everyone scattered into small groups to talk, I cornered Flynn to make sure he was staying with Alyssa the whole weekend. With her not quite due but far enough along to pop at any moment, I didn't want to take any chances.

He narrowed his eyes in suspicion. "Why me?"

"Mum will be around as well, of course," I said, "but Lys is being stubborn about not needing help, so she won't let Mum stay. But she'd never dream that I'd ask you to be my eyes and ears on the ground, so that's exactly what I need you to be. Pretend you're there to watch the race. Claim to have had too much to drink. I don't care what you do. I just want someone at home with Lys and Pheebs in case Lys goes into labour. Knowing her stubborn arse, she wouldn't call the ambulance because she doesn't want to inconvenience the drivers. I wouldn't put it past her to try to drive herself to the hospital through her contractions."

The closer her due date drew, and the bigger her stomach became, the more obstinate she was about not needing help. She'd spent ten minutes trying to pick a pair of nail clippers off the floor, refusing help from both Phoebe and me. It would have been endearing if it wasn't so fucking frustrating.

He laughed. "You're not wrong. I think if things hadn't gone south so quickly last time she would've been the same."

"If anything goes even the slightest bit wrong, I want her in an ambulance and then you call me. Have you got that?"

"Yes, sir." He grinned at me. "You know, I like this commanding, protective version of you way more than that dickhead I met at Emmie's graveside."

I snorted as I recalled my behaviour leading up to that meeting. "Yeah, me too."

"I'll work my magic with Lys, and your wish shall be my command." He went to move back to Alyssa's side.

"Oh, one more thing," I said, drawing his attention back to me. "If something happens and I can't make it back in time, make sure the right name goes on the fucking birth certificates this time, yeah?"

A bark of laughter left him. "Sure thing, Dec. Good luck in the top end."

As it grew later and the party wound down everyone left, saying their goodbyes to the birthday girl and wishing me luck for my race.

I just hoped my little boy would hold on until I got home again.

AFTER EVERY session on the track, the first thing I would do was get my mobile phone and check for news from home. I was a fucking nervous wreck. Thankfully instead of distracting me, it was almost as if I was able to channel the frustration into the car to give it a few extra Ks an hour. It put me on pole, then first in the first race. Everyone kept saying that if my form kept up, there was every chance I'd be able to claw back to third or maybe even second in the championship.

Still, it took everything in me to focus on the track and not think about Alyssa and Phoebe at home. Whenever my attention strayed to them, I reminded myself that they were the reason I was racing hard. Keeping the team going, keeping the team and driver rank positions strong, would benefit our family in the long run.

The moment the race meet was over, I ensured everyone had everything under control and then was on a plane heading back home. There would be time to celebrate my overall win later—once I was certain Alyssa was safe and the baby wasn't going to be born without me at her bedside.

Thankfully, there'd been no movement at the station when I arrived home, but she did have another antenatal appointment booked for the following day that I'd be able to accompany her to.

As a way to celebrate a belated birthday, Phoebe and I had a daddy-daughter day at the kart track. Because she was now five, she was able to go on the tandem karts and I could show her the fun of speed.

As we flew around the corners, she squealed and giggled.

"Can I go by myself?"

"Not yet, sweetheart," I said. "But one day, I'll show you how to beat every other sucker out on that track. Does that sound good? Coming first, just like Daddy."

Wide-eyed, she nodded. After a moment, she asked, "Can we go fast again now?"

Even though I'd only planned for the one session, I couldn't resist her little hands coming together to beg or the pleading pout on her lips.

"Let's do it."

WITH NO urgent need for me to be in the office, and Alyssa's due date so imminent, everything non-vital was put on hold. I went to work only when absolutely necessary—leaving the team to each do what they did best. Because I was desperate not to miss a thing and ensure that everything was ready for Brock's homecoming, I had Mum on constant standby to pick Phoebe up from school if something happened.

I hovered around Alyssa so much I was certain she was getting sick of me. The first pregnancy with me at her side was highly likely to lead to our divorce. Even my upcoming birthday wasn't important in the grand scheme of things.

"I can do it, Dec!" she snapped at me when I bumped her away from the chest of drawers.

She'd spent the better part of the morning cleaning and sorting everything out in the nursery before deciding that it might be better to change the floor plan and move the chest of drawers away from the change table so that Brock wouldn't be able to move from one surface to the other when he got a little older. Why it couldn't be moved later, I had no idea. Or even why it couldn't be the change table—the piece of furniture that was on fucking wheels—that was the one to be moved.

That wasn't to be, though.

Instead, Alyssa had decided it *had* to be the chest of drawers that moved so it could rest against a different wall. I was going to be damned if I let her be the one to shift it, though. As I dragged the heavy-as-shit furniture around, Alyssa jumped on the other end to try to help me. I opened my mouth to tell her to buzz off and just supervise from a safe distance when she went pale.

"Oh shit," she muttered.

"What is it?" I raced to her side in a minute but stopped short when I saw the small puddle of water at her feet. "Oh shit!" My exclamation was far louder than hers. "Is that . . .?"

She nodded. "I think my water just broke."

"Fuck, we've gotta get you to the hospital. Get in the car."

She laughed as she held up her hand. "It's not that—" She winced and stopped talking—something she'd been doing for the better part of the morning. "It's not that big of a rush," she finished a moment later. With the information about her broken waters playing in my head, I had one question.

"Fuck, Lys, have you been having contractions all morning?"

"Maybe. I wasn't sure. They started a few days ago, but the pain's been getting worse."

"Fuck. Fuck. Fuck." I was trying to calculate the travel time into the city. I'd seen movies; it was all such a rush. "We need to get you to the hospital. Now!"

"Relax. It's not that—" She paused again for a moment. Her fingernails bit into her palms. "That big of a deal. I'll call the hospital and see if they want me yet."

"Are you fucking crazy? We need to move. Now. You already want to try the VBAC thing. There's no way you're doing that here. I can't have your uterus rupture here. I wouldn't know what the fuck to do." I paced the room and dragged my hands through my hair. Why wouldn't she just get in the car? Didn't she know precious minutes were ticking by?

I figured maybe she'd move quicker if I got her hospital bag organised for her, so I left the room without another word and ran to the room where her bag was all packed up and ready to go. By the time I had it in my hand and was back at the door to the nursery, Alyssa was on the phone.

"I understand," she said. "Yep, no worries at all. We'll see you soon." She met my worried gaze. "Actually, wait, can you just repeat that to my husband?" She laughed. "Yeah, something like that." She held her phone out for me.

"Hello?"

"Sir, I've just advised your wife that it's probably a good idea for her to come to the hospital at her convenience to be examined. It sounds possible that she's in early labour. The most important thing is to not panic and not stress. There's likely to be a long way to go yet."

My mind just churned over the words early labour over and over. Fuck, I needed to get her to the hospital. If I didn't . . . If something went wrong that could have been avoided by taking her there sooner . . .

"We'll be there as soon as we can!" I hung up the phone as soon as the words were out. "You heard the lady, Lys. In the car."

"No."

"What the fuck do you mean 'no'?"

"I'm not going anywhere right now. I want that chest of drawers in place first, and I'm not leaving at all until you've calmed down."

"Calmed down? *Calmed down*? You're in labour, Lys. I can't exactly be calm. We. Need. To. Get. To. The. Hospital." I emphasised each word to ensure she understood. Maybe the pregnancy brain was impacting her ability to reason and think logically.

When she still didn't move, other than to wince again, I dropped the bag and moved to the dresser, shifting it to the wall she'd determined it would be best on. A string of curse words was on my lips as I moved.

"There. Now can we go?"

"At my convenience, Dec. It's likely to be hours and hours before anything happens."

"But—"

"No buts. I want to clean up this mess and then we can go."

"Fucking hell," I muttered under my breath but dutifully grabbed some rags to clean up the fluid on the carpet. Alyssa disappeared and came back with the Bi-Carb Soda. Just like she had the night Phoebe had been sick at our old place in Sydney, she sprinkled some around.

"We can vacuum that up later," she said, glancing around the room in a quick once-over before giving her nod of approval. "Give me a minute and I'll call your mum from the car to get her to pick up Phoebe and bring her home."

"You're not going to have her bring her to the hospital?"

"What part of 'it might take hours' don't you understand? It's not like the movies, Dec. There's not some mad rush to get to the hospital because the baby is minutes away. Phoebe will be bored out of her mind."

Rationally, I knew that. I'd experienced it with Rose and then heard it from Morgan. But the rational part of my brain wasn't in control. The part of me that wanted to have Alyssa hooked up to every medical device just to make sure there was nothing wrong with her, or with Brock, was in charge. And he wanted to get Alyssa to where the doctors were in the fastest possible way.

"Besides, I've already called the ambulance. The hospital wanted me to travel with them, just to be on the safe side." Her words were a reminder that her delivery was high risk because of the issues she'd had the last time and because she wanted to attempt the VBAC.

I begrudgingly agreed to wait until they arrived.

When the ambos came, Alyssa finally got a move on and went with them without question. She was all smiles and laughter as I tried to hurry her up before grabbing her bag and jumping in the car to follow them.

It was nearly an hour later before we were finally at the maternity ward of the Royal Brisbane Hospital. They assessed Alyssa and then, after confirming what Blind Freddy could probably see—that she was in fact in labour—led her into the birthing suite.

That's when everything seemed to stop. The midwife came in from time to time to check on Alyssa's progression, check Brock's heart rate with the Doppler, and just generally ensure everything was okay, but that was it. There were no rushing beds sliding through the doors of the hospital corridors. No doctor sitting at the end of the bed waiting to catch the baby when he came. And no blue drapes that seemed to feature in every movie.

Through it all, there was one constant: the helplessness that took hold in my chest. My gaze fell on Alyssa so often, and each time she looked almost serene, no matter what she was doing. Even as her contractions grew stronger—to the point where she was gritting her teeth and squeezing my hand each time—she didn't complain that it was too much. I wondered whether part of that was because she didn't want to be forced to have a C-section again if she made too many complaints.

"You're doing really well," the midwife said on her next visit—after we'd been there for the better part of six hours. "You're about eight centimetres dilated. Soon it'll be time to push."

I stood at the side of Alyssa's bed and brushed the hair from her face. The effort she was going through, the strain she was hiding, was clearer up close. Her skin was coated in a light sheen of sweat. Once she had the all-clear, though, she paced the room again.

Less than half an hour later, Alyssa's obstetrician came in to introduce herself again. Apparently, the "high-risk" nature of the birth meant Alyssa was to be closely monitored by a doctor throughout the next stage.

As Alyssa's labour progressed, so did her stress. The laughter, smiles, and cute little winces stopped, replaced by groans, hand grips that could have popped open a tin can, and a near permanent sheen of sweat on her brow.

"How are you going?" I asked, for probably the eighteenth time since we'd got there. I hated being so useless. There wasn't much I could do but rub her back whenever she stopped pacing the room and offer what comfort I could with my presence.

She grabbed my arm. "Ask me that one more time and you'll be the one needing to lie down."

I pressed my hand over hers and bounced my leg. "I just wish I could do more for you."

"I think you've done more than enough," she muttered after another contraction had hit her. They were almost permanent, one running into the next into the next. "Get the doctor. I need— Get the doctor now!" she roared before gritting her teeth.

She didn't have to tell me twice. I pushed the call button while she climbed back onto the bed.

The doctor and midwife came in moments later to check on Alyssa.

"I feel like I need to push," Alyssa said as the doctor assessed her before announcing that Alyssa was fully dilated and the baby was crowning.

"It won't be long now," the doctor added. "Everything looks good with the baby's heart rate and he doesn't seem to be under any stress."

"I need to push!" Alyssa cried again as her hand closed tightly around mine. She squeezed so hard her knuckles were white and my fingers lost all feeling.

The doctor encouraged her to follow her instincts. When she did, her hold on my hand impossibly tightened. A feral growl ripped from between her clenched teeth and her heels dug in to the sheets. Even after she'd exhaled all her breath, she kept pushing until she fell back against the bed, panting and exhausted. More words of encouragement came from the doctor about how well Alyssa was doing.

"You're doing great, baby," I murmured as I leant closer to her to brush her hair away and kiss her temple.

I pulled away and glanced down at the doctor, buried between Alyssa's legs. Then I saw it.

Our son's head.

Holy shit.

"Holy shit," I repeated aloud as my smile grew. "You're doing so great."

Another contraction hit. Another near torturous grip on my hands. Another feral grunt through Alyssa's gritted teeth. And then sweet music: the sound of a cry, piercing and quiet all at once.

Then our baby was placed on Alyssa's chest and I couldn't breathe. He was so small. So tiny and so helpless. I looked up at my perfect wife and grinned as tears rushed into my eyes. The midwife and the doctor were still busy and still talking, but I couldn't hear any of the words.

I was transfixed by the sight of Alyssa and Brock together. Fuck. How could I ever have not wanted this? How could I have thought my life wasn't heading in this direction?

"Look what we did, baby," I muttered as I met her eye.

"Dec," Alyssa prompted as she reached out to pat my cheek before nodding toward the end of the bed.

The nurse was waiting for me to say something. I gave her a little apologetic smile to tell her I wasn't sure what I'd been asked.

"Would you like to cut the cord?"

I nodded even though the thought sent my pulse racing. My hands shook and my mouth was dry. As I cut the cord, my gaze found its way back to Alyssa and Brock. There was something missing, but after Alyssa was settled into the ward, I'd go home. Then I'd return first thing in the morning with Phoebe, and everything would be complete.

It was only when I was driving home, a few minutes after midnight, that I realised it had just ticked over to my birthday. Brock had been spared sharing my birthday by just a few hours. Still, a new healthy baby and a safe delivery for Alyssa were all I'd wanted for my birthday. There was nothing more I could have asked for.

CHAPTER NINE

FAMILY FRIENDLY

EVEN THOUGH WE'D already been a family—I'd already been a father—nothing had prepared me for the arrival of a new baby. He screamed all night; shit almost constantly; and when he wasn't eating, screaming, or shitting, he was sleeping. Still, I was enamoured with him.

And Phoebe adored him. She'd often sit on the couch under Alyssa's watchful eye holding her baby brother. Phoebe would cradle Brock's head carefully like she'd been shown and sit with him while watching TV.

A little over a week after he was born, I had to head off to Townsville. I'd asked Alyssa multiple times whether she wanted me to cancel and whether she'd be okay, but each time she all but shooed me out the door. Still, both of our mothers knew Alyssa was alone, so I was sure she'd have plenty of extra hands and lots of support—probably more than she really wanted.

Of course, I left armed with photos of him, him with Phoebe, him and Alyssa, and photos Mum had taken of our whole family.

The last ones were the ones we'd released to the media to keep them off our doorstep.

I took to the track like a man possessed. I'd never been more in control or ready to win than I was during that weekend. Winning for my family was the best way I could think of to honour them. Not that they'd care if I came last, but it gave me a reason to race harder than ever.

When I came home, the first thing I did was grab a screaming Brock off Alyssa and tell her to take some time for herself. She was a fucking trouper, and I was more than willing to do my share of the child wrangling.

At least until Brock shit in his nappies with something akin to toxic waste. Then . . . well, then I would have been more than happy to hand him back to Alyssa, except she'd locked herself in the bathroom and wouldn't open the door.

Fuck.

With my shirt pulled up over my nose in an attempt to block out the smell, I managed to get his nappy off. Almost the second the air hit his dick, he pissed all over the change table, himself, and the nappy I'd grabbed for him.

"Fuck," I muttered as I tried to clean up the piss while keeping one hand on Brock so he didn't somehow wiggle himself off the change table.

"Phoebe!" I cried. "Can you come here please?"

She was at my side in a moment. "Yes, Daddy?"

"Can you please get me towels? And a nappy for Brockie?" I could have asked her to watch Brock while I got everything else, but it seemed more responsible to put the five-year-old in charge of the inanimate objects.

While I waited for Phoebe to get back, I wrestled my shirt off and wrapped it around Brock so he wouldn't get too cold.

"Here you go, Daddy," Phoebe said, handing me a tea towel. Rather than telling her to try again, I just dealt with it. God, I didn't know how Alyssa did this so many times a day.

Then again, even though I was covered in piss, in a room filled with the lingering scent of toxic-waste-dump-style shit, and half naked after sacrificing my shirt to the greater good, I was still happier than I had been drugged up and balls-deep in any stranger.

THE REST of the race season passed in a blur until Bathurst was on me again. The last few times I'd raced at the mountain had all been vastly different. One had almost seen my career decimated. At the time, I would have thought my life was over, but that event brought Alyssa back into my life.

The next had restored not only my career but had cemented my place at my family's side and had seen the conception of our son.

And the third time, well, despite coming sixth in the 1000, I was so fucking happy. It was a respectable finish considering it was me and a super-rookie driver tackling the race. Just getting through the race cleanly was an accomplishment. It cemented Emmanuel Racing as the team to watch.

Alyssa, Phoebe, and Brock had even come with me. Flynn had accompanied us, ostensibly as our babysitter but he spent just as much time rubbing shoulders in the pits and with the celebrities on track. Something told me he could get used to hanging out with some of the talent. At least he took Brock and Phoebe off our hands for the night before the race so Alyssa and I could relive the life we'd had the previous year. It was a good chance to reconnect with her as a fucking gorgeous woman and not just a domestic goddess.

After that weekend, the rest of the year slipped away until Christmas approached again. Things had been crazy, and more than a little hectic, but I wouldn't have changed a single day of it.

When I came home from the staff break-up party at Emmanuel Racing before the Christmas holidays, I was more than ready to relax and spend some time with my family. Although I would have liked Alyssa to go to the party too—she was as important a member of the team as I was—she ended up staying at home because she'd been too sick to go. Between the vomiting bug she had and running around after two kids, she was exhausted. I would have avoided the party, but being the team owner and lead driver, it was one of those times I had to suck it up and do whatever was needed of me.

When I walked in Brock was fast asleep in Alyssa's arms, stretched out with his arms above his head. His little pout sucked on air as he slept. Already six months old, and he was getting so big. Taking in the bags under Alyssa's eyes, the slight frizz in her hair, and the fact she looked more than ready to nod off, I went to grab him off her to let her get some rest, but she shook her head.

"He's only just drifted off," she whispered. "I don't want to risk waking him."

I brushed my hand over her hair before kissing her forehead. "Are you sure you're okay?"

She nodded and gave me a watery smile. The joy in her eyes was there, just buried a little under her sleep-deprived weariness. "There's something on the bed for you, though."

I frowned as I wondered what it could be.

"Just try to keep it down when you open it, okay?" she added as I turned away. "However you feel about it."

My frown deepened as I headed down toward the bedrooms. Before I went to our bedroom, I looked in on Phoebe in hers. She was fast asleep, curled around her pillow with a smile on her lips. I moved to her bed and kissed her temple. Time went by too fast. It was hard to believe we were only a few days away from our third Christmas together.

The four of us had made it through what was sure to be the craziest year of our life. After all, we knew what to expect from team ownership now, and Alyssa kept telling me that babies got easier as they got older. As much as I'd loved the last year, I was ready for life to settle into something a little calmer.

Leaving Phoebe's room, I found my way to the master bedroom. On the bed was one of Phoebe's shoeboxes with a note stuck to the top that read, *Are you ready for this?*

While my mind turned over the question of *ready for what?* I flipped open the lid. When I saw what was inside, I dropped the whole thing back onto the bed. The blood drained from my face and I couldn't believe what I'd seen. Unlike the previous Christmas, I didn't need to look twice to figure out what Alyssa's gift was—or what it meant.

I found my way out to the living room with the words *holy fuck* running over and over inside my head.

"Surprise," Alyssa whispered when she saw me coming. It was hard to know how she was feeling about it. "So are you? Ready for it?"

The information settled over me slowly. The two lines on the stick. The confirmation that our little family was going to get that much bigger once again. Another baby on the way. As it really registered, my smile grew.

"Yeah. I think I am."

The words didn't seem strong enough to convey the growing certainty in me that it was exactly what I wanted. Despite the fact that she was exhausted, a little frazzled, and ready to collapse, Alyssa was the perfect mother. She was as stunning as ever, and my love for her grew with every single day. The truth was, now that I was faced with the reality of having to do it all over again there wasn't a single regret in my mind. Maybe I would've liked a year off, but it didn't matter that my choice had been taken away by fate. I was ready.

If she wasn't holding my son, I would've picked her up and spun her in my arms.

A grin was plastered on my lips as I said, "Actually, I can't fucking wait."

THE END

PHOEBE REEDE IS BACK!
HERE'S A TASTE OF HER STORY

Chapter One

Breakout

THE PHONE IN my pocket vibrated again, seconds before the not-so-dulcet tones of my favourite band blared from the speaker. I bit my lip and walked faster as I ignored the call.

Again.

Fuck. Dad was going to go mental when I finally answered. And that was nothing compared to how he would react when he found out where I was and where I was going.

In the time since I'd arrived at the airport, I'd counted no less than fifteen text messages and three phone calls already. If only he could chill and back off for a little while. It wasn't like I was planning on avoiding him forever. Only long enough that by the time he learned of my plan, it would be too late for him to do anything to stop me.

In an attempt to shake the feeling of dread stealing through my limbs, I focused on the flight ahead. I tugged my phone out of my pocket, being extra careful not to answer it accidentally, and checked the time. Ten minutes left to check in. After that, I had another half hour before I would be able to board.

While I made my way to the check-in desk, I scrolled through the missed calls and texts on the silent-for-now phone. Dad's tone had grown less patient with each text. I checked the one sent minutes before the call I'd ignored.

Call me now.

I rolled my eyes. Seriously, it was like he expected me to disappear in a puff of smoke if I didn't report back every hour. I looked at the time again and weighed my options. If I gave him too much notice of my intention, he might still be able to call in some favours and cancel my flight. I had to wait until the last possible moment.

"Checking in for the Sydney flight," I told the lady behind the check-in desk when it was my turn.

She gave me a polite smile that held no warmth. The sort that was guarded and full of judgment as her eyes roamed my face. Well, fuck her. It wasn't my issue that she was too old and crusty to appreciate the streak of pink in my mahogany hair. Filling my gaze with challenge, I levelled my stare at her. People like her didn't intimidate me. Little did. It was hard to be intimidated by small-minded people when you grew up like I had—surrounded by cameras and misogyny.

My phone beeped again. Ignoring the lady—it wasn't like she was paying me any attention anyway as she went through documents with a fine-tooth comb—I checked the new message.

Call your father, please, Phoebe?

Mum. Damn. It was getting serious now. Dad was bringing out the big guns.

Now that she'd gotten involved, there was going to be twice the trouble when I finally did call back.

Fuck it.

I blew out a breath and replied to her. Or stalled her at least. *I'm in a movie. I'll call Dad when I'm out.*

The snooty cow behind the check-in desk gave me another once-over before placing my boarding pass on the desk between us and insincerely wishing me a safe flight.

"Fuck you very much," I said with the sweetest smile I could muster before snatching my pass and yanking my carry-on up from the scales and onto my back.

My phone chimed. Dad. Again.

I know you're not at the movies, Angelique called here for you. Where are you?

It was damn tempting to ignore the message, just like I had every other time the phone had gone off, but I couldn't keep ignoring it much longer, or Dad would call the police. And the Coast Guard.

Fuck, knowing his overprotective arse, he'd probably call Interpol, the FBI, and the KGB despite the fact they were all in different damn countries.

The overprotective streak he'd had since turning up in my life when I was four only seemed to be growing thicker as my eighteenth birthday approached. It was possible he was experiencing some sort of advanced empty-nest syndrome or some shit.

My four younger siblings should have been enough to stave that away—Nikki, the youngest, was only eight months old after all—but apparently not. True, Nikki had been a late surprise for Mum and Dad, but looking after her should have been enough to keep him off my case.

But no. It had left him three times as clingy.

Maybe it was the fact that Nikki had been born sick, like I had been, and reminded him of the fact that he hadn't been there to support Mum when my twin brother, Emmanuel, and I were born. Or maybe it reminded him of the statistics surrounding my life. Survival statistics that looked bad on paper but none of us dwelled on because it was more important to live and take care of myself than to worry about any potential for future issues. I didn't know. All I knew was that I needed space. More than anything, I needed to get out of the fucking house for a while.

I was too many things to too many different people, and I was fucking sick of it.

When I found my way to the gate, I pulled out my phone and dialled a number I should have called long before this point. Would have, if I didn't think she'd have warned Dad of my plan.

"Hey, Pheebs, what's up?" Eden's voice wiped away the tension that was building in me. She was great like that. Even though she lived in a different state, she'd always been the one I could turn to when I needed to talk. She'd never driven a race car, but she'd had her start around the track—almost as young as I had—working with her uncle, my dad's former boss. She understood the track and the misogynistic pigs that I'd had to contend with ever since I'd started racing in karts. The vulgarity I heard at the track. The general boys' club attitudes I faced every day.

"I'm coming to visit," I said as I lifted my legs onto the plastic seat opposite me and slunk down in my own. It was far easier to give a "fuck-off and don't talk to me" vibe that way.

"Terrific. When?"

"My plane leaves in twenty minutes."

"What?"

For the first time, I worried that maybe she'd say it was too much of a hassle, and I shouldn't bother. That she'd revoke her permanent invitation. "You don't have to pick me up. I can get a cab."

"You're coming today?"

A nervous chuckle slipped from my lips. "C'mon, Aunt Edie, I thought you were faster than this. Yes. Today. Now."

"When were you planning on telling me?"

I chewed on my lip for a moment. "About now."

"What if I wasn't here?"

"It was a risk I had to take. I had to get out of the house."

"And do your parents know you're coming here?" She had her take-no-shit tone on. I had to win her around, or I was going to have as shitty a time at her house as I was having at my own.

"They will."

"Uh-huh."

"Honest, Aunt Edie, I'm calling them as soon as I get off the phone to you. Cross my heart."

She sighed. "Your dad is going to kill me. You know that, right? He's not going to believe that I wasn't part of the conspiracy."

"You worry too much. Dad is a pussycat really. He just needs to learn when to back off."

"Did you two fight again?"

I sighed and flicked my head forward, playing with the chunky pink strip in my hair. "He just doesn't get it."

"You might be surprised what he would get if you'd talk to him about it."

"He hid the keys to my bike." It was what had finally pushed me over the edge. Three days earlier, he'd taken them from my bedroom and cut me off from my one escape. It was a fucking betrayal—especially after all I'd done for him and Mum lately.

"What?"

Unable to contain the frustration anymore, I stood and started to pace the length of the row of seats. "Said it was a fucking death trap. I mean, the guy's made a living out of racing cars, but heaven forbid I jump on a Ducati."

She chuckled. "He's just worried about you. He doesn't know bikes."

"It's not like Flynn and Luke would've given it to me if I didn't know how to handle it." Flynn had been a surrogate father to me for the first four years of my life and Luke was his partner, an actor who had been a rising star when they'd met and was gaining bigger and better roles under Mum's management.

Although Dad had stepped readily into the role of fatherhood when he came back into Mum's life, Flynn had never really backed off completely either. Of everyone, he was the one most likely to keep my secrets and let me get away with stuff. He was the only one who knew about the way I'd circumvented the rules to get my bike licence.

"I know, baby girl, but that won't stop your dad from worrying. He knows the safety of a ProV8 car first-hand. It's not like your bike has a roll cage."

I didn't need her trying to convince me of the many reasons why I shouldn't ride my bike as well. She was just like Dad when it came to cars versus bikes. They just didn't get it. "I thought you'd understand."

"I do, but I also think you need to consider your dad's point of view."

"Are you going to be home or not?" On my next pacing lap I met the gaze of a teenage boy watching me walk. He nudged his friend as his eyes trailed the length of my leather pants before lifting to cop another eyeful of my boobs. The cotton T-shirt I wore did nothing to accentuate my C-cup, but it did nothing to hide it either. Great. Either they recognised me or were regular run-of-the-mill teen perverts. I needed to figure out which one if I was going to deal with them properly.

Eden sighed again. "What time does your flight get in?"

I gave her the details before hanging up, relieved that she'd come around in the end. Not that I'd doubted it. She'd always been there for me.

Once I'd hung up, I kept my phone in my hand and prepared myself for the next phone call. The one I was dreading the most. Anything I said—any explanation I gave—would disappoint Dad, and I hated that thought. I despised doing things that made him anything other than proud, but I needed to get away from his shadow for a while.

From the whole situation at home.

My finger was on the Call button when I heard a voice behind me.

"Excuse me?"

I turned and met the eye of teen creep one. "Yeah?"

"Are you . . ." He trailed off and looked at his shoes.

When he lifted his gaze to meet my eyes again, he gave a shy smile. There was no doubt the colour of my irises had confirmed his question long before my words ever could. After all, comments about my unique turquoise eyes that were "just like my dad's" were probably the second most common thing I'd heard.

"Are you Phoebe Reede?"

And there's the first.

For a long time, it had been, "Are you Declan Reede's daughter?"

But over the years, as I'd started to make my way through the classes in karts and production cars, I became a little more known in my own right. Especially among boys my own age. After all, I was a walking wet dream for them. It didn't matter what I looked like, what I wanted in life, or what my passions were. All that mattered to them was I had boobs and the ability to drive.

And without wanting to sound like a braggart, put me near an engine and I could make it sing. It didn't matter what. Two wheels to eighteen, I was always in perfect control.

Of course, the tabloid sensationalist stories about my apparent stream of boyfriends didn't help either. So many guys thought I would be an easy score, which only added to the interest.

Arseholes.

Unfortunately for the raging hard-on posing as a normal kid in front of me, I had no patience for those attitudes after everything I'd been through. I drew myself up to my full height and clenched my fists. "What's it to you?"

"Whoa, sorry I asked." He raised his hands in surrender and walked away.

Yeah, keep walking, buddy.

I might have been good with cars, bikes, and trucks, but wasn't nearly as good with people. I didn't need to be. They didn't keep me company during the hours at the race track. Only the motors did that. People tended to be a source of disappointment in the long run.

Knowing I'd sufficiently kept the oglers at bay, I pushed the Call button on my phone. It didn't even ring twice before Dad's voice came down the line.

"Where the hell are you, young lady?"

"Hi to you too, Daddy."

"Don't 'Daddy' me. You had your mother worried sick; where are you?"

I scoffed. As if it were Mum who'd been worried. He just couldn't admit that he'd been panicking. "I went for a ride."

"I thought I told you that you weren't to ride that bike again."

"Yeah, you did. I just didn't listen."

"Where are you, Pheebs?"

"Out." I'd intended to tell him my plans when I'd called, but his over-the-top reaction pushed the right buttons to make me bite back rather than cooperate.

Before I could say anything else, or get him off the phone, the first boarding call for my flight sounded over the loudspeakers at the airport. It was the warning that they were seating business class and families, but the advantage to flying on the company dollar was that I could book business.

"Are you at the airport?" Dad's tone told me I'd be in a lot of shit when I got home, but it didn't matter. All that mattered was getting away. At least for a night or two.

"I'm just going to see Aunt Edie. I've already arranged it with her."

"And when were you planning on telling me? Or your mum?"

"Now?" I'd been able to say it with some authority when I'd said it to Eden, but the anger in Dad's voice disarmed me. "I'm sorry. I just need some space. I'm nearly eighteen; I can't be in a house full of kids."

It wasn't like I hadn't lived with Eden before on and off, usually around race meets that would take me to Sydney for a few weeks. I even had ID with her address on it . . . which was how I'd been able to get around Queensland's tighter rules for getting a bike licence. No way was I going to wait until I was eighteen to even apply.

"Phoebe, please, come home? We can chat about what you need—"

"I will. I just need this first, okay? Love you." I hung up the phone while he was still talking.

For the first time since I'd planned my getaway, I debated not following through. Audrey, the travel clerk at Emmanuel Racing, would probably get in some shit over the fact that she'd booked me a flight. Again. It wasn't like she'd broken protocol this time. After all, she'd been told not to book anything I asked for, but Dad had never forbidden her from booking flights in my name that came from his email. Not even emergency bookings with less than twelve hours' notice.

I was sure there would be another tightening of the procedures now that I'd found the loophole and hacked his emails.

Another tightening of the noose around my neck.

My phone started to ring again, but I rejected the call and turned off my mobile entirely. I slung my bag over my shoulder and headed onto the plane. I'd deal with the fallout of my decision when I came back home, just like I had every other time I'd run away.

Check out
Phase (Phoebe Reede:
The Untold Story #1)
for more.

ABOUT THE AUTHOR

Michelle Irwin has been many things in her life: a hobbit taking a precious item to a fiery mountain; a young child stepping through the back of a wardrobe into another land; the last human stranded not-quite-alone in space three million years in the future; a young girl willing to fight for the love of a vampire; and a time-travelling madman in a box. She achieved all of these feats and many more through her voracious reading habit. Eventually, so much reading had to have an effect and the cast of characters inside her mind took over and spilled out onto the page.

Michelle lives in sunny Queensland in the land down under with her surprisingly patient husband and ever-intriguing daughter, carving out precious moments of writing and reading time around her accounts-based day job. A lover of love and overcoming the odds, she primarily writes paranormal and fantasy romance.

Comments, questions, and suggestions for improvements are always welcome. You can reach me at writeonshell@outlook.com or through my website www.michelle-irwin.com. Thanks in advance for your correspondence.

You can also connect with me online via
Facebook: **www.facebook.com/MichelleIrwinAuthor**
Twitter: **www.twitter.com/writeonshell**

Made in the USA
Columbia, SC
04 March 2018